בית ספר גבוה בית יעקב דשיקגו

Bais Yaakov High School of Chicago

3550 West Peterson Avenue • Chicago, Illinois 60659

Yesterday's Child is a powerful story of a family that is drawn closer to each other and closer to the Creator by an unexpected crisis. It is presented to you by Bais Yaakov High School of Chicago, the newest link in the golden chain of Torah education for girls started by Sarah Schenirer in Poland over seventy years ago and continued by Rebbetzin Vichna Kaplan in America. Bais Yaakov, headed by Rebbetzin Shulamis Keller, herself a student of Rebbetzin Kaplan, is dedicated to inspiring its students with *emunah, bitachon* and selfless dedication to the Torah.

The school's goal is to develop a *derech hachayim,* a Torah sense of direction, which will help prepare the girls for the vast and varied experiences of life. This is to be achieved by internalization of all that is studied into the character, emotions and actions of the *talmidos.* A dedicated staff of dynamic, experienced and committed teachers offers a high-level educational program, both in Torah and in general studies. Individualized personal attention is given to each girl in order to help her develop her maximum potential. An extensive vibrant program of extracurricular activities is designed to develop useful skills and talents and to make the girls' school experience more enjoyable and fulfilling.

Your support will help develop today's young Jewish girl into tomorrow's *aishes chayil*—woman of valor.

Yester-day's Child

Yester-day's Child

a novel by

Ruth Benjamin

Published and distributed
in the U.S., Canada and overseas by
C.I.S. Publishers and Distributors
180 Park Avenue, Lakewood, New Jersey 08701
(908) 905-3000 Fax: (908) 367-6666

Distributed in Israel by
C.I.S. International (Israel)
Rechov Mishkalov 18
Har Nof, Jerusalem
Tel: 02-518-935

Distributed in the U.K. and Europe by
C.I.S. International (U.K.)
89 Craven Park Road
London N15 6AH, England
Tel: 81-809-3723

Book and cover design: Deenee Cohen
Typography: Nechamie Miller
Cover photography: Solaria Studios

ISBN 1-56062-176-1 hard cover
1-56062-177-X soft cover
Library of Congress Catalog Card Number
92-73911

PRINTED IN THE UNITED STATES OF AMERICA

with thanks to:

Rabbi Yisrael Shusterman

Rabbi Nachman Meir Bernhard

Rabbi Dr. Moshe Singer

Rabbi Yaakov Yosef Reinman

Raizy Kaufman

Yehudis Gralnik

Leah Saban

and special thanks to the
Johannesburg Beth Din.

One

The ambulance flew along the South Coast road of Natal, its sirens screaming, its lights flashing. The stillness and darkness of the pre-dawn hour seemed to accelerate its urgency.

To the left were the occasional lights from the houses of people who could not sleep in total darkness. To the right was the sea, inky black against the sky. Was there the suggestion of approaching dawn?

In the ambulance lay a young woman. Her face was a dusky red, almost purple, and beads of sweat stood out on her forehead. She was wearing an oxygen mask, and her breathing was very heavy and labored. Next to her on the monitor, her heartbeat traced its unsteady way in luminous green across the screen.

A doctor with a sense of urgency about him was adjusting her intravenous infusion, a paramedic assisting him.

In the corner of the ambulance, seeming to almost shrink into its walls, was a twelve-year-old boy. His face was chalk-white, his hair blue-black in comparison. His green eyes were wide with terror, and he kept biting his lips to keep them from trembling out of control.

His name was Anthony, and the woman lying on the stretcher, looking so different from the woman he knew as his mother, was Mrs. Sylvia Isaacson. A shiver ran through the boy. Maybe it was too late. Perhaps he should have called the doctor sooner. His mind went back to the evening before. Was it only a few hours ago?

"Tony, please get me a blanket to put on top of this quilt. The weather must be changing. It has suddenly become very cold."

Anthony frowned. He was still perspiring from the heat of the day, and it had been a scorcher. As far as he was concerned, it had hardly cooled down at all. He would certainly not be able to sleep with anything warmer than a sheet.

Nevertheless, his mother was shivering and coughing a little as he went to the cupboard in the hallway. He stood on a chair to reach the top shelf where the blankets had been stacked at the end of the winter. He brought one down and went to his mother.

She smiled at him gratefully.

"I'm sorry, Tony, I will use it later. I don't feel so cold any more." Her face suddenly contorted into a coughing spasm. Why was she coughing like this?

"What's the matter, Mum?" he asked. "Are you feeling all right?"

"Oh, it's just a bad cough, I think," she said. "Maybe I have a slight temperature. It's nothing important."

"Can I get you something, Mum? Something to make you feel better?"

"Maybe you could get me some Eno's antacid and some

of my headache tablets. I will take two."

He gave them to his mother and pulled the quilt over her.

"It's hot, Tony. Perhaps you could get me a cool sheet."

He again opened the hall cupboard and brought one to her, and sat at the end of the bed, watching her. She turned to him. Was she feeling better? She certainly did not look well. Her breathing seemed heavy, and she was wheezing slightly.

"Did you finish all your homework?" she asked. At this very effective dismissal, he went out of the room, saying he would be back. He did have an English essay to write. English was his favorite subject.

At the school he was attending in Port Shepstone, they had just recently become very strict with homework. He looked through the essay subjects. He had already picked one he liked best, "If only I could fly." He sat and thought, chewing the end of his pen as he did so.

He started as he heard his mother coughing and wheezing from her bedroom. He went in and she looked at him reassuringly.

"Don't worry, Tony, I didn't mean to interrupt you. The painkiller will work very soon. Are you going to do the essay about flying?" She seemed to have some difficulty in breathing.

"Yes, Mum," he said uncertainly. She closed her eyes and he left the room, but he found he could not concentrate. He walked over to the lounge window, pulled aside the lace curtains and looked out at the sea.

The sea always seemed to calm him, even when it was night and he could hardly see the white foam on the dark waves. He was quite happy in their tiny apartment, furnished simply but tastefully, and kept spotlessly clean by his mother. He was especially happy in summer when all the vacationers came down to the coast in droves, filling up every cottage and apartment with brightly-clothed people sporting surfboards and snorkel gear. Out of season it was quiet, but then he could enjoy the walks along the sandy paths close to the sea, and watch the waves smash against the rocks in a futile attempt to dislodge them.

The influx of vacationers meant that his mother was constantly busy in her curio shop. At peak times, he would spend several hours a day assisting her. Business would be thick and fast, in sharp contrast to the quiet, out-of-season days when no one would come into the shop for hours.

He sat down on his bed, which folded up into a couch during the day. Would his mother be all right? Should he call the doctor?

He walked back to the bedroom and he looked at her in the light coming in from the lounge. The expression on his mother's face and its dusky color made him very nervous and uneasy.

She was sleeping, however, or she seemed to be, because she did not respond to his call.

He walked out uncertainly and sat at his desk.

"If only I could fly." Why couldn't he think of anything to write? He had had so many ideas about it during the day.

With difficulty, he finished the essay, eventually falling asleep.

He was awakened by loud, almost animal-like groans and ran into his mother's room. Her face was a deep, bluish red. She was panting, trying to catch her breath, and she appeared drowsy. Though she tried, she could not speak to him. There was no question at this stage about calling the doctor. He fumbled with the tiny alphabetical notebook, their personal telephone directory, until he had found the doctor's number. Then, feeling as if all his fingers had become thumbs which were shaking like jelly, he dialed the number. The doctor had been there within minutes. An ambulance was called from Port Shepstone, and they were on their way at high speed to the Addington Hospital in Durban. The doctor had said it was not too late, but that he never knew Anthony's mother to be asthmatic. He had said that he needed the best-equipped intensive care unit.

Anthony didn't once take his eyes off his mother or off the screen beside her. He knew that the green jagged lines were something to do with her heartbeat, but who knew what they really signified!

Suddenly, the beeping stopped and the machine sounded an alarm. Both the doctor and the paramedic seemed to spring into a rush of activity. They were putting something on his mother's chest. The luminous lines appeared to have gone out of control. The doctor put electrodes on her chest to try to shock her heart back into life. Her body convulsed, and Anthony watched with a horrified fascination, feeling that some movement, any movement, even something as gross as this, meant that she was still alive.

Following this was consistent, almost feverish activity on the part of both medical personnel. They put down an endotracheal tube, which made Anthony feel sicker than ever. He was frozen with horror, but somehow he became aware of a change in the buildings around him, the lighted streets and the traffic lights. He stared out the window. They were in Durban City. Addington Hospital was minutes away. His mother would be fine. Hospitals always helped.

He breathed a sigh of relief as he saw the hospital gates and as the ambulance went through, still at top speed, to the emergency department.

Everything, then, seemed to happen so fast. The ambulance doors were pulled open from the outside and his mother's stretcher yanked out; the doctor and paramedic following with drips and machines held high. He was ignored completely as they rushed her through the reception area into emergency.

By the time he was able to collect himself sufficiently to follow, she was nowhere to be seen, nor were the doctor or the paramedic.

Everyone seemed to be too busy to talk to him, especially the nurses and doctors who might have been able to help.

He sat on a chair with relatives and friends of other patients and eventually managed to work out that the nurse behind the desk seemed to be the one person who had an idea of what was going on in the emergency area.

He walked over to her, explaining that his mother had just arrived in an ambulance.

She pointed to white swing doors.

"They are busy with her now," she said. "Sit down and wait."

He went back to his seat. He was going to be very, very tired in school the next day. No–it wasn't even the next day, it was that day, today.

His eyes were beginning to feel heavy when the doctor came out through the swing doors, spoke to the nurse and walked over to him.

"Anthony," he said. "I can see you are very tired, and we want you to sleep for a few hours."

"My mother," he stammered. "Will she be all right?"

"She is resting," he said. "There is nothing you can do now. I would like you to sleep."

"Can I see my mother?" he asked. "Can I just give her a message? Is she awake?"

Nobody seemed ready to answer any of his questions, and he followed the nurse to a side ward. She then said something to the doctor about a social worker and left, returning with a cup of cocoa which he drank gratefully. His mind was racing and bursting with a million questions, but eventually he fell asleep.

Two

Something about the social worker's tone of voice unnerved Anthony. Why was she speaking to him so carefully, so sympathetically, and yet why were her words evoking within him waves of panic, fear and nausea which kept rising at the base of his stomach and shooting up towards his throat?

He had been awakened half an hour earlier by a hyper-efficient nurse who had drawn the curtain sharply and told him he had better wash and eat breakfast quickly, as the social worker was coming.

His heart had sunk as he remembered where he was, and he had turned to the breakfast tray and nibbled disinterestedly at some fruit. He did not feel up to the rather lumpy looking porridge that had been served to him, a grayish white island topped with sugar, floating in a sea of milk. At the best of times he hated porridge, especially lumpy porridge.

He hoped his mother would not have to stay too long in the hospital, but even as he thought this, another, more panicky feeling had overtaken him. What if she were to die?

Die? Of course she would not, could not die. His mother was strong and quite young, and only old people died . . . at least usually. She couldn't die because she had so many things to do, besides be his mother and look after him.

He had tried to force the thought out of his mind. It had kept forcing its way back, making him feel more and more that sense of cold fear and panic.

Why couldn't he turn the clocks back to yesterday, when they had been shopping together in the supermarket, trying to work out what was on sale that day? How normal and natural everything had been; her only worry was how to make her tight budget stretch a little further, his, to do his homework on time.

She couldn't die!

The social worker was a nice young woman, impeccably dressed, wearing a metal, oblong disk which labelled her as "Shelly Hanson, Social Worker." She had been out of university for one year, and was still finding her feet in the profession. She had, however, a natural sensitivity and she was finding it difficult to be in her present situation with Anthony. A sense of helplessness was enveloping her.

Again, the boy asked the same question, and again she brushed over the subject.

"Will my mother be all right? Will she die? She can't die, can she?"

"Don't worry about that now," she said, knowing that the truth would inevitably have to be told.

"I need you to give me some details about your family. In the meanwhile, don't you want to eat?"

He made a wry face at the porridge.

"You don't like porridge, do you?" she said, sympathizing with him. She hated porridge, especially lumpy porridge. Would it be unprofessional to admit it?

"It's lumpy, and anyway, it's cold now," he said.

"I'll try and see if I can do something," she said, having a vision of taking him to the canteen and buying him a toasted cheese roll. But that definitely would not be professional. And she did need some information.

"Please give me your names again," she asked. "No one has filled in all the details."

Almost mechanically, he told her his name, his mother's name, his address, telephone number, mother's place of work, school, birthdays, and so on.

When she came to "religion" and he answered "Jewish," her face brightened.

"Ah, that's a solution," she said, and excused herself from the room.

A few minutes later, she was back with another tray, this time labelled "kosher." The offending porridge was removed.

"I am not religious," Anthony said.

"That doesn't matter, does it? You are Jewish, so we can order kosher food for you."

"I am not sure if I have ever eaten kosher food before," he said, breaking the seal and looking curiously at the dishes beneath the covering.

Mmm . . . it smelled good. He was soon eating hungrily as if he hadn't eaten for weeks. The social worker smiled, but then her anxiety returned. How was she to tell him?

In the meanwhile, she needed a lot more details, and she knew it would be almost impossible to get them afterwards.

She started chatting to Anthony about his mother, about life on the South Coast, about his mother's work, his school, his friends. Every so often she would write something down and he wondered vaguely why she was doing this.

Now she needed details about the father. She hoped, for his sake, that there was a good relationship between them.

"You said that your mother was divorced," she began. "Do you know how long ago that was?"

"Yes, of course," said Anthony. "It was almost nine years ago." His voice had become a little flat.

"Do you seem him often?" she asked. "Does he visit?"

"He's in Cape Town," said Anthony. "I haven't seen him for four years." His face started to flush, but he tried to keep his voice unemotional.

"He is married again. He married almost immediately after the divorce. He's got other children, now, a boy and a girl."

"But you are his eldest son, aren't you?" she asked.

He could contain himself no longer.

"He doesn't care about me, or us. He couldn't care if we lived or died. He wouldn't shed a tear if we starved in the street, or if we went about in rags. He has someone else now, a new family. He has thrown his real family into the gutter!"

The social worker realized that these were the words of the mother, probably repeated regularly to the boy. Even in her short experience as a social worker, she had heard these themes repeated often by children pouring out fury in adult tones and language.

"But he sent you money regularly, didn't he?" she asked, wanting somehow to defend the boy's father. She had to make him look better in the child's eyes.

"Oh, yes," he said, still repeating what he had heard so often. "Every month regularly: a loveless, puny check would be put in my mother's bank account. It wasn't enough for anything. My mother had to slave away to put me through school. There wasn't even enough money for decent sneakers."

"Didn't you spend holidays with your father?" she asked. "I mean, he must have had a right to some contact with you."

"Oh, yes," he said. "For the first four years. I saw him every year for about three weeks. At first he would come and fetch me in the car, but then, after his children were born, he would get my mother to put me on the train in Durban and fetch me at the station there. But my mother asked him to give us the money rather than the train fare, and anyway, I didn't like him at all after what he did to us. I didn't want to see him. I wanted the extra money for my mother."

The social worker gave a sigh. Would single parents ever learn not to bias children against their other parent? The parent's own hatred and hurt made situations like this so difficult.

"So, you don't really know him?" she asked.

"He used to phone a lot," he said. "He still does. But I haven't really spoken to him much. His wife tries speaking to me also, but I can't speak to her. How can I? She took my mother's place."

"Your father and his wife tried to keep contact with you, and you didn't want it," said the social worker quietly.

"Who would want to keep contact with *them*?" he said, in disgust. "My mother and I were perfectly happy together. We didn't need anyone else. And do you know what?" he said, his eyes suddenly filling with tears. "Do you know what? This year he completely forgot my birthday. I watched and watched the post, but nothing came, not even a card. He just totally forgot." He was crying freely now, a confused, hurt expression on his face.

"Did he always send you presents for your birthday?" she asked.

"Oh yes! Every year," he said. "He really sent good ones. On my last birthday, the one before he forgot, he sent me a really fantastic computer game, an expensive one."

"What did your mother say about your not getting a

present?" she asked, expecting him to repeat a torrent of abuse.

"Nothing," he said, "absolutely nothing. She just said something about next year." He frowned. Yes, that had been unusual.

"Did you ever phone him?" she asked.

"Yes, sometimes if we needed something, like the time I needed money for camp. Mum said I should phone him."

"He gave it to you?"

"Yes, he posted it straightaway," he said.

"Do you know his number offhand?" she asked, as casually as she could.

"Yes, I do," he answered. "I even know his work number." He gave her both numbers, and she wrote them down.

"I will be back in a minute," she said to him. "I just have to arrange something for a patient of mine."

With that she was gone. Why did she want to know so many things about him? Why was she writing it all down? And she hadn't told him how his mother was, and how long she would be in the hospital. He would ask her as soon as she came back.

"Did you ask anything about my mother?" he asked. "Is she feeling better? Can I see her?"

The social worker sat down again, not really knowing what to answer.

"I will find out for you soon. I will ask the doctor," she said. "In the meanwhile, we must just get some more details."

She asked him who his minister was, or, rather, his rabbi.

He explained once again that though they were Jewish, they were not religious, and that he had never really met a rabbi. There just weren't any on the South Coast of Natal. "But," he added, "soon I will be *bar-mitzvah*. I am twelve now, and in eleven months' time, I will be thirteen. That's a very,

very special birthday, and you have got to do a bit of religion or something for it. My mother will contact the rabbi in Durban for me. I think his name is Rabbi Green. We hadn't contacted him yet, because it's months and months away. I have to do a blessing or something in the synagogue."

"Who is your best friend at school?" she asked.

"My friend? Oh, Stephen of course," he said. "He lives in our apartment block. His mother is also divorced, but his father comes to visit quite often. He never . . ."

They were interrupted by the doctor walking into the room and speaking quietly to the social worker.

As he went out, he gave Anthony a strange, compassionate look, which evoked the fear inside of him all over again.

The social worker had turned white, and she did not seem to know what to say to him. Had something dreadful happened to his mother? The waves of fear were beginning to take hold of him again.

"Anthony," she said, finally. "Anthony, the doctor just phoned your father and spoke to him. He is catching the first plane down here to be with you."

A cold numbness seemed to settle itself firmly in his chest. Something was desperately wrong.

"But . . . but why?" he stammered.

"You father wants me to tell you," she said. "Your mother . . . she . . . she's . . ."

"She died!" shouted Anthony. "She is dead! Where is she? My mother is dead! No, she isn't . . . She isn't dead, is she?" He started to cry and scream as the social worker nodded, and then he suddenly stopped, left with a cold numbness and a feeling as if he had been kicked hard in the chest. The social worker put her arms around him, and he started to cry again, this time with heavy sobs, sobs which seemed to wrack his whole body. His life was finished! He couldn't live without his mother!

"Are you sure?" he asked, over and over again. "Are you absolutely sure?"

The doctor came in, asked him to lie on the bed and gave him an injection. He fell asleep almost immediately.

Three

David Isaacson stood uncertainly, watching his sleeping son. He was a tall, dark-haired man, with almost a duplicate copy of Anthony's large, green eyes. He, too, was white-faced, and his hands shook as he straightened his tie.

"You . . . you really have told him, Miss Hanson?" he asked, unaware that he was asking the question for the fourth time.

"Yes," she said. "We told him a few hours ago, and then we gave him an injection, and he went to sleep."

"And he does know I am coming?" he asked, this time for the second time.

"He knows that," she said again.

"Did he . . . did he talk about me?" He looked more uncertain.

"We did talk," she said, hesitantly. "We talked before we told him about his mother. I gather you haven't really had much contact."

"My ex-wife poisoned his mind against me. We weren't

given a chance to be father and son."

He stopped, realizing that he had heard these same words on perhaps a dozen television programs.

She, too, had heard these words on at least a dozen television programs. But it was, unfortunately, a reality of life.

"I understand," she said. "That often happens."

"He didn't really want to talk to me," he continued. "Sometimes he spoke to me as if I were an enemy. I felt I wasn't really needed or wanted by that family, except for the money, of course, and I was always careful with that."

The social worker sighed. What hadn't been portrayed on the television screen was how much a child needed the non-custodial parent, how important it was for a father to persist, despite the antagonism, until he gained the child's affection, in spite of what the other partner might say. It was not the time to mention this now. A doctor entered briskly.

"Mr. Isaacson, please sign these forms." He handed them to him, indicating where he should put his signature.

"Was there . . . was there nothing that could be done?" he asked.

"Nothing at all," said the doctor. "It was a fatal asthma attack. Her heart stopped in the ambulance, and they managed to get it going, but when it stopped again about an hour later, there was nothing we could do to revive her."

"So, it's finished," he said. "I can't believe it."

The doctor left the room, leaving him with the social worker and the sleeping boy.

"I must speak to him, mustn't I?" he said, looking nervously at his son. "Or, perhaps I should just wait until he wakes up."

"Perhaps you would like to go to the canteen and get yourself some coffee, and something to eat. He will be here when you get back."

The man breathed a sigh of relief for the brief respite, and left the room.

The social worker turned to the child. Yes, it must be very, very difficult to come and fetch a son whom you hardly know, a son who was full of antagonism, a son whose mother has just been snatched away in a flash. The father was obviously very shocked. Perhaps she could make it easier.

"Anthony, wake up," she shook him. "It's Miss Hanson, the social worker. Your father has just gone to the canteen to eat something. He won't be long."

Confused and a little groggy, Anthony woke up. He immediately remembered his mother and a look of intense pain and shock creased his face.

"She's dead, isn't she?" he whispered. "It wasn't a dream, was it? She is dead."

"Yes," said the social worker. "Your father is here."

"I don't want to see him," he said. "He won't understand how I can miss my mother. He hated her."

"I am sure he didn't hate her," she said. "He looks very shocked."

"It is probably because now he has me on his hands," he said resentfully. "I will come and interfere with his new family. I would rather go to an orphanage!"

As he said these words, the tears started to fall like huge, heavy raindrops, and he sobbed and sobbed.

His father walked into the room, saw his son crying, and spontaneously held the boy in his arms.

He could not think of anything to say, so he kept quiet, holding him and stroking his hair.

The boy was too unhappy and desperate to resist, and it was, in fact, a comfort to have his father's strong arms around him. He was far too miserable to resent him. Was it going to be easier than they had thought?

But no! Anthony suddenly stiffened and his father stepped backwards.

"You can't really feel sorry for me, you don't really love me," Anthony said. "You just want me to be quiet so that you can take me home with you, and then send me off to boarding school as soon as possible. You don't really want me."

"Oh, Anthony, I do, I do," said his father, who was also crying. "Please don't say that, son. I know it is hard for you, but it is hard for me also. I want to look after you."

Anthony looked at him for a few seconds and then gave a long sigh.

"What does it matter?" he said. "Everything is finished, with Mum gone. Are you sure she's gone?" He turned to the social worker. She just nodded.

"With Mum gone there is nothing left, nothing to really live for. Why couldn't we have both died together in a car crash or something? Then I wouldn't be alone! Why didn't she wait until I was grown up? Then it wouldn't have been so bad. Why now?"

He started to sob and cry again and once more his father put his arms around him.

The social worker left, saying that they could call her if they needed her.

After a while, Anthony calmed down."When are you going back to Cape Town?" he asked his father.

"*We* will be going back in a couple of days," said his father. "We have some things to settle in the hospital about the funeral. We also have to go back to the apartment and . . ."

Anthony again dissolved into tears.

"How can I?" he asked. "How can I go back there? I would *die* if I had to go back there."

"I will take care of it," said Mr. Isaacson. "Are there any friends you can stay with while I pack up the apartment?"

"Stephen," said Anthony. "I could be in his apartment, and then you could phone me and ask me if you have problems with packing."

"Do you know anyone who might be able to help me pack up?" he asked.

Anthony looked blank.

"All right," he said, "I will speak to the caretaker."

"Mrs. McNeally," said Anthony. "She looks after the building."

"We will phone her from the hotel so that she knows what is happening," he said.

Several hours later, they left the hospital, and went to one of the beachfront hotels after buying Anthony a change of clothes. Mr. Isaacson made several phone calls, calls which made Anthony feel sick, but which he realized had to be made, including lengthy calls to the *Chevrah Kaddishah* both in Durban and in Cape Town.

Afterwards, father and son took a walk along the shore.

"Can I tell you something about Cape Town, Anthony?" began his father. "Can I tell you about your . . . your family?"

"*Your* family," said Anthony deliberately. There was an awkward silence.

"*Our* family," said his father, at last. He did not wait for a reply. "You met my wife, Sheila, a long time ago. She is really looking forward to seeing you and to having you with us."

Even as he said this, his words sounded hollow, but he continued.

"And we have two children, as well as you," he added. "As you know, Debby is seven and Jules is five, nearly six."

"He was a baby when I saw him last," said Anthony. "I remember him, and I remember Debby as well. She ate all my ice cream out of the cone when I wasn't looking and then just smiled at me. She was very sweet!"

For a few seconds he almost felt good, but swiftly the bleakness returned.

"But she is much older now, isn't she?"

"Yes," said his father. "They are really looking forward to seeing their big brother."

It almost sounded as if it wouldn't be so bad, but Anthony still felt surges of antagonism. This man, the man who was now offering him a home, didn't even send enough money for sneakers, and hadn't remembered his birthday.

He was beginning to feel quite tired, and he had a cold, empty feeling inside his chest.

What did the future hold? How old was he? Only twelve. Soon he would be thirteen. Suddenly he remembered.

"Dad," he said, "I am going to be thirteen soon and I think I need a *bar-mitzvah*. Maybe I should go to a rabbi."

"That's no problem," said his father. "We will arrange all that. We are regular synagogue-goers; we go at least once a year, on either Yom Kippur or New Year, whichever is more convenient. We will find someone."

They heard a siren quite close to them, and the scene of the ambulance ride and of his mother's last few hours came back to him as if with terrifying reality. He whitened. He felt as if his head and his heart would burst. He could bear it no longer.

Suddenly he saw an arcade with computer games, for which his father quickly handed him some money. Anthony went over to one and played with a frantic concentration, trying to absorb himself in the battles and in the chase.

The ambulance scene left him.

He came back to his father. Maybe he wasn't so bad after all. But no, he had hated him for years, and would continue to do so. Loving him would be disloyal to his mother.

"Anthony," said Mr. Isaacson as they were going up to the hotel room, "what did you buy with the money I sent you for your birthday?"

Anthony stiffened. What money?

"Your mother must have been really surprised to see so much on the maintenance check, but I explained to her that it was for you."

Four

Anthony knew he could not really avoid the trip down the South Coast to the apartment to help his father. There were books he had to return, and things he had to pack away carefully. His father would be selling the furniture, and asked if he particularly wanted to keep anything. He had pointed to his small desk, reminding his father that he had bought it for him.

When they entered the apartment, Anthony cried when he saw his mother's bed in such disarray, his finished essay on his desk. Somehow, he managed to sort through his things, at times having to shut his eyes against the memories.

At one stage he had become a little braver and began to feel a little better. He was surprised that he was feeling numb, surprised that he could look for a few seconds at his mother's picture. He decided to take a picture of himself and his mother to keep near him always. It was a framed snapshot taken on vacation years before, when he had been just a little boy. But then a wave of terror and grief overcame him, and he lay down on the bed, his eyes shut, hot tears pouring out beneath them. His father sat down on the bed beside him and stroked his hair, but Anthony became stiff and rigid.

It would take time. It would really take time.

They worked for several hours, until a van came and collected the furniture, leaving only the packed boxes and the desk, and other things they were sorting out from the cupboards.

It was already dark when they finished. The desk, several large boxes and a trunk stood ready for the railway transport to collect the next morning, under the supervision of the caretaker, Mrs. McNeally. She had also offered to arrange for Mrs. Isaacson's clothes to be given to charity, a suggestion that had come as a relief to both father and son. The clothes would be removed, and they would benefit someone else.

As soon as he went back into the hospital where his mother had died, Anthony felt a heavy black cloud envelop him. He wanted to leave this place, and forget it forever. He wished he had not insisted on accompanying his father. He could have remained sleeping in the hotel. His father would probably have returned before he was even awake.

But he had insisted, as if driven by an inner morbid fascination to see the place once more.

Now he wished that he had said nothing. Was it really only two days since he had been here? It felt like a lifetime had passed in these two days.

But it was the hospital, especially the emergency department, that was now disturbing him so deeply. Where was his mother? What had they done with her? He knew his father had arranged for her body to be railed down to Cape Town, so they could have the funeral there. Was she still in the hospital? Somehow he knew she wasn't.

His father was directed to an administration office where he had to sign more papers and collect the death certificate.

It was a relief when he came out and once again they were on their way to the hotel. They would be catching a plane to Cape Town at midday.

Anthony had never flown before, and he could not help but feel a little excited at the thought of being in the air. If only the heaviness and aching would leave his heart, even for a moment. Would he be living with this for the rest of his life?

Watching the land and the sea beneath him on the plane was exciting, and he asked his father countless questions, most of which Mr. Isaacson, being a civil engineer, had been able to answer.

As they approached Cape Town, however, Anthony was seized with nervousness. How would the new Mrs. Isaacson relate to him? His mother had told him that a stepmother always resented a stepson and daughter. If that wasn't true, where had all the fairy stories come from about wicked stepmothers?

As if reading his mind, his father spoke. "Your stepmother and the children will be meeting us at the airport."

Anthony withdrew into himself. He was not sure how he was going to relate to his new family. He became sullen and silent.

Even the incredible scenery of the majestic Table Mountain and the two oceans which lapped at Cape Town's shores didn't lift his mood.

He remained polite but cool as he met his stepmother. He did not really mean to be like this, but somehow he could not respond to the woman who had ousted his mother from her rightful place. He could not remain cool to the greetings of the children, however. They were obviously thrilled to have a big brother, and they hugged him and chatted to him.

Debby kept telling him about her new doll which he *had* to come and see, though of course her other doll had nicer hair, but he could decide.

He nodded in agreement, responsive up to a point, but feeling somewhat awkward. He was not used to children. He had had friends of his own age group and had met the women of his mother's age group. They had not socialized much, if at all, with families with small children.

The drive from the airport was quite long, and he looked out of the window for most of the way, responding listlessly to the children's questions.

He began to think about the money his father had sent with the maintenance for his birthday. Had his mother not realized it was his money? No, his father had said he had made it clear. He knew she had been financially pressed, and that the money would have helped with many household things. But surely she could have told him, and then borrowed it from him. He would have lent it gladly. He could not understand.

A wave of guilt swept over him. How could he think like that about his mother? His mother was dead now. Dead? Even as he thought about it, the word sounded strange. What did it mean? She was just not there any longer. Where was she? Was she completely gone? She had been alive.

He searched his pockets for some tissues. He could not let his stepbrother and sister see him cry, he just could not. But the tears just came and Jules put his head on his lap and Debby held his hand. Mrs. Isaacson handed him some more tissues without comment, only a sympathetic glance. Anthony was grateful for her silence.

They turned off the highway and down a quiet street. There they stopped. Anthony knew they had moved since his visit to them four years ago, but he had not expected their new home to be such a large house in such a fancy area. It might be rather nice to live here.

But no, again his mother's voice seemed to ring accusingly through his brain. His father was living in luxury with his new family, while he and his mother had lived in a tiny apartment, having had to struggle for everything, living on his puny maintenance. He began to flush with resentment, but he found it going away as Debby and Jules led him to the room which was now to be his own, an upstairs room with new matching curtains and quilts in various shades of blue, with ships on them. There was also a bookcase, containing suitable books for a boy of his age, a hi-fi set and well chosen pictures, mostly of the sea and of ships, on the wall.

Mr. Isaacson, who had been following the children into the room, turned to his wife.

"How did you manage to do all this in three days? You have really made it into a boy's room. I am impressed!"

"It was fun doing it," she said. "It will be really good to have Anthony here. I will have a friend I can talk to."

She doesn't mean it; she can't mean it, said Anthony to himself. She is a stepmother, and stepmothers can't be trusted at all. At the same time, he had to admit, he was more than impressed with his room.

"I was going to get you a desk, Anthony, but I heard that yours is coming from Durban. We put a little table here in the meanwhile. You can work on that," she said.

Work? Oh yes, he hadn't thought about that. He would have to go to a new school, catch up on all the work.

"Maybe you would like to unpack, Anthony," said his father, bringing in the cases.

He started to do so, assisted by every member of the family, one by one.

The day became evening and then night. His feelings of

depression were becoming stronger. He excused himself, saying that he was ready to go to bed.

The children looked at him strangely. Surely his bed-time could not be before theirs. Jules immediately went to his room, rummaged in his toy cupboard and pulled out a fluffy, blue, woolly dog.

"For you to sleep with," he pronounced, giving it to his big brother.

Anthony took it and looked hard at Jules. The child looked so familiar. Where had he seen him before? He had only known him as a very, very young baby. Then, even through his depression, he smiled. Of course, the photograph album. Jules looked exactly as he had done in so many of the pictures. Debby, on the other hand, with her clear blue eyes and honey colored curls, looked very much like her mother.

He got into bed, and, telling everyone he was very, very tired, put the new quilt over his head and cried himself to sleep.

It rained on the day of the funeral. Everything was muddy and wet and as the rabbi read the prayers and spoke about his mother, Anthony watched the rain collect on the brim of the rabbi's hat and then trickle off down his jacket.

How could he be making a speech about his mother? He had never even met her! He didn't know her at all! How could he!

Was it really his mother in that coffin? It couldn't be. How could it be? His mother was somewhere else, surely.

As they walked to the newly dug-out grave, their shoes squelching in the mud, Anthony felt a sense of unreality. Who was in that box? It must be an old, old woman, someone who had died after five hundred years. It could not be someone he knew, someone who had been so young, so vibrant, so alive.

As he heard the hollow thud of the mud being thrown onto the coffin, he imagined that they were planting a tree, a tree in a forest, but he shuddered as his father tried to pass him the spade. He was not having anything to do with planting that tree! And who were all these people? Who *were* all these people? He did not know any of them, except of course his father and stepmother. Why had they all come to his mother's funeral? They didn't know his mother, did they?

And yet, they all followed them home, and they all had tea and all greeted him with sad, solemn faces, and then turned back to one another, chatting happily. Did any of them really care? Why were they there? Did they know or care about the searing pain in his heart that seemed to have settled there forever? Were most or maybe all adults so false?

Jules came in and hugged him, somehow sensing his desperation. Did he care? He was only a child. Were children perhaps more sensitive, more caring?

But he didn't understand. Could he understand? Of course not. But he felt Anthony's hurt and responded to it. One thing he did know: the sun, for him, had eclipsed forever.

He would never be happy again!

FIVE

It was six weeks later. Anthony still awoke at five o'clock every morning to the sound in his mind of the ambulance sirens and of his mother's heavy breathing. At other times, it was the hollow thud of the mud being thrown onto the coffin.

The searing pain, however, had abated, to be replaced by a dull ache and a constant headache between his eyes.

The first day at school had been traumatic. As a new boy arriving mid-term, he had minimal chances of being accepted immediately. This, together with his intense grief and withdrawal, made him a very lonely boy.

He longed for Stephen or for someone he could have spoken to. After wandering alone around the recreation field for a few recesses in succession, he obtained permission from the teachers to stay in and catch up on the work he had missed in the first part of the term. For the first time, he actually liked his schoolwork, and the teacher, noting this, helped him considerably.

But his heart ached for his mother, his old school, his

apartment. His fantasies took him back to the curio shop, back to the customers. It seemed as if his mother would appear around the corner, give a reassuring smile, and tell him it had all been a nightmare, that he would awaken at his desk to see his essay finished and his mother telling him to go to bed.

But reality was cold, hard and uncompromising. His mother was dead, somewhere in the cold, wet ground, in a box. He was living with his father and stepmother, people who up to this point, had almost been his enemies. Enemies? They didn't really *behave* like enemies. Really, he could see that they had made quite strong efforts to be friendly. But it couldn't be sincere, could it? How could it be sincere?

Perhaps with his father it was sincere, because he was, after all, his father. But with his stepmother, it couldn't be. After all, didn't all stepmothers resent children from a first marriage? His mother had always told him that.

And their living standards! They were far above what he and his mother had had to endure. It just proved that his father was not interested. They had just managed to survive!

He could find no rationale at all, however, for the children being so fond of him, and he had to accept that this, at least, was sincere.

At times, Jules would follow him around with a kind of hero-worship, imitating his every action and looking up with his large, green eyes to see if Anthony approved. Debby would wait for him to arrive home from school, and take his hand and show him her drawings and paintings and chat endlessly to him about the dolls in her doll house.

In many ways, he was becoming used to his new environment, and he had to admit that at times he even liked it.

There was none of the constant struggle for every rand that they spent. He had a garden he could play in, and his room, especially with his desk inside it, had become a haven to him.

When he felt happy, however, he felt guilty. How could he be disloyal to his mother?

He began to worry about his *bar-mitzvah* lessons. Would his father remember to arrange them? As far as he knew, except for the funeral, his father had not gone anywhere near a rabbi or a synagogue.

One day, Anthony broached the subject shortly after his father came home from work.

Mr. Isaacson sighed. "Sheila, what do you think we should do? Would you be able to take him to those *bar-mitzvah* lessons?" he looked inquiringly at his wife.

"I suppose so," she said. "It depends what time they are. Where would he have to go?"

"Well, I suppose to the Great Synagogue," said Anthony's father. "That's where we go on New Year or *Yom Kippur.*"

"It's quite a distance from here," she said thoughtfully. "Isn't there something nearer?"

"Yes," he said. "I think there is a synagogue only a few streets down. Perhaps you have passed it? Oh no, you never go that way, but I have. I don't know if it's Reform or Orthodox or whatever, but I don't think that matters. They all do these things."

"Do they have a rabbi?" Sheila asked.

"Well, I suppose so, they must. It definitely is a synagogue; it had a star of David on it and some Hebrew writing. And I suppose that synagogues always have a rabbi. Actually, it looked quite nice," Mr. Isaacson mused. "Not like the Great Synagogue, of course, but in fact, quite homey. Maybe they are a bit more relaxed than the big one. I mean, this idea of not being allowed to smoke there is quite inconvenient, especially when you are fasting for a few hours. They should be more considerate. Maybe this synagogue is better."

"And I could walk there after school," said Anthony. He much preferred not to have to be too dependent on his stepmother.

"Thank you, Rabbi Levy, for seeing us. We would have made an appointment, but we didn't know your phone number, so we just dropped in on the off-chance," said Mr. Isaacson, looking a bit flustered. He wasn't used to rabbis. They always made you feel guilty for whatever you were doing or not doing.

"This is my son, Anthony. He needs a *bar-mitzvah*, and it is getting urgent. He will be thirteen in only six months' time."

The rabbi nodded, looking at Anthony quite intensely for a few seconds.

"Would you like to leave him with me for an hour or so?" asked the rabbi. "I would like to talk to him about what he knows already about Judaism."

"Well, I shouldn't think he knows much of anything," said his father. "His mother . . . she passed away a few weeks ago . . ." his voice trailed off.

The rabbi looked again at Anthony, this time with a look of understanding.

"His mother died, and she wasn't very religious," Mr. Isaacson continued. "We are more religious and we go to synagogue at least once a year, but she was never interested in that kind of thing. But I think we have come in time. How much would the lessons be, and when should he come to you? When are the classes?"

The rabbi smiled. "This is a small synagogue and we don't have a *bar-mitzvah* class as such."

"Oh, I'm sorry to hear that. Please tell me where the

nearest class could be found," said Mr. Isaacson, preparing to leave.

"No, I will teach him myself," said the rabbi.

"I am not sure how much we can afford for private lessons," his father said. "I mean, how often do you want him?"

"Well, I want him fairly often," said the rabbi.

Mr. Isaacson started to go red. He was not going to be taken advantage of. These rabbis . . .

"There will be no charge," the rabbi said.

"Not at all? Why not?" asked Anthony's father. "We can afford it."

"If you would like to make a donation to the *shul* after the *bar-mitzvah*, you are welcome," said Rabbi Levy. "But it is up to you. In the meanwhile, I will speak to Anthony for a few minutes, and also introduce him to my son Yaakov, who was *bar-mitzvah* a few months ago. Yaakov will be able to help him a lot."

He turned to the boy.

"Can you read any Hebrew?" he asked.

"No," said Anthony. "Do we have to do that?" He looked thoroughly alarmed.

"Listen, I don't want you to put too much pressure on him," said Mr. Isaacson. "We just want you to do the ceremony. But I suppose it is good for him to be able to know the Hebrew alphabet. I even remember some of the letters myself." A dreamy expression came over his face.

The rabbi ascertained Anthony's Hebrew birthday and his *bar-mitzvah Parshah*, and then asked him his Hebrew name. The boy looked blank and looked at his father.

"Given at the *bris*," said the rabbi. "He did have a *bris*, didn't he?"

"Oh yes, of course," said Mr. Isaacson. "We did have him

'done.' We had quite a few people there."

"You gave him a Hebrew name then," said the rabbi.

"Yes," he said. "I just can't think of it at the moment. I knew it began with 'A' because it had to be like 'Anthony'. In Hebrew it was the name of an animal, I think . . . a tiger . . . or maybe . . ."

"A lion? Aryeh?" asked the rabbi.

"That's it!" said Mr. Isaacson, looking pleased. "That's exactly it. I remember now. How could I have forgotten?"

He rose to leave, leaving Anthony with the rabbi, the boy reassuring him that he would find his way home.

"Perhaps we could go to my house," said the rabbi. "It is just next door, and you can meet Yaakov, and my wife can give us something to eat."

Anthony was surprised at how comfortable he felt in the Levy's house. Sara Levy, the rabbi's wife, was a particularly warm, caring person, and when she heard of the boy's loss, her innate compassion was instinctively aroused.

Anthony liked Yaakov immediately, but was somewhat in awe of him. After all, he wore a *yarmulka*, and was obviously very, very religious. But then, he had to be, because his father was a rabbi, and religion was his job.

Obviously, Anthony could never be friends with a person like Yaakov. They were worlds apart. Yaakov probably thought only about religious things, and definitely would have no interest in sports.

He noticed that even Yaakov's younger brothers wore *yarmulkas*. How strange it all was. Would they wear them outside in the street, or at the shops? And what were those strings sticking out from under their shirts? Were they also religious things?

"Come, let's talk, Aryeh," said the rabbi. The way he said his Hebrew name sounded good, but again a little strange.

That wasn't his real name, or was it? He was Anthony.

The two of them sat together in the lounge. On a little table to Anthony's right stood a large glass of fresh granadilla juice and a small plate of biscuits. He looked at the rabbi, and suddenly, to his extreme embarrassment, he found large tears rolling down his cheeks. He put his head in his hands.

"I am sorry," he said. "It is just . . ."

"I know," said the rabbi. After all, didn't much of his work consist of counselling people in various kinds of trouble? "You have been through a very bad time."

The boy continued to cry. The rabbi handed him a box of tissues.

"I am sorry," said Anthony again. "Maybe I should just go and come back another time."

"What's going to happen to all that granadilla juice and the biscuits?" asked the rabbi, joking gently.

Anthony smiled through his tears. He was beginning to like the rabbi.

"Do you want to tell me about it?" asked the rabbi softly.

"Well, my mother died, and now I am with my father and my stepmother, and I miss my mother and our apartment, and . . . everything!"

Slowly, at first, the story emerged, eventually coming out in a torrent of words and tears. He told the rabbi about his essay, the ambulance, his mother's breathing, the social worker, his father's birthday present to him—everything that had been gnawing at his heart and mind over the past few weeks.

Eventually he stopped and drank half the juice.

"We didn't speak about my *bar-mitzvah*," he said at last. He blew his nose hard.

"Do you want to talk about it now, or shall we leave it for tomorrow or the next day?" asked the rabbi.

"Isn't it urgent?" asked Anthony.

"Yes, it is," said the rabbi. "But I can see you are a bright boy, and if you come to me quite often, we can take care of it."

"Shall I come every day after school?" asked Anthony eagerly.

"Let's say for a start, every Monday, Tuesday, and Thursday after school," said the rabbi.

Anthony drank down the rest of his juice and quickly finished the biscuits.

"It's Monday today, so I'll see you tomorrow," he said. He stood up, rubbing his eyes.

"Can people see I've been crying?" he asked.

"Perhaps you should wash your face before you go," said Rabbi Levy. "By the time you get home no one will notice. You can always say you have a cold."

The boy smiled. "I keep saying that at school," he said. "Everyone thinks I have a terrible allergy."

If the Isaacsons noticed that Anthony had been crying, they made no comment. He had determined, on his walk home, not to think about his mother, and had spent his time doing his homework in his head. Also, he had been met at the door by an enthusiastic Debby and Jules, and had gone to play with them until suppertime.

Later that evening, while he was busy with his homework, Sheila had come into the room, asking him how it went with the rabbi. He replied enthusiastically, and though she was pleased about this, she felt inexplicably uneasy. She pushed off the feeling, telling herself that she had no reason to feel this.

As she was about to leave the room, Anthony stopped her. "Sheila, do you know anything about this kind of algebra?" he asked.

She came back and looked at the page. Relieved that she remembered it, she helped him with his homework for the next half hour.

Perhaps it would not be so difficult after all, she thought.

Six

The *bar-mitzvah* lessons were going well. Rabbi Levy realized that Anthony knew absolutely nothing about his heritage, and he and his son worked out a "crash course" in Judaism which would give him at least the basics of what a *bar-mitzvah* really meant. Rabbi Levy wanted Yaakov to teach Anthony *alef-beis*. He had watched his son help his younger brothers and sisters with their homework, and it was obvious that he could teach. He knew it would be beneficial for both boys.

Almost as soon as the rabbi started teaching Ari (as he was always called in their home), he realized that he was responding differently than his previous students. This boy had a real interest, a deep interest, and was not regarding it as a chore. He absorbed information like a sponge.

Rabbi Levy also realized very soon that Ari was not treating the *mitzvos* he was teaching him as intellectual exercises that he had to learn, as the other *bar-mitzvah* boys had done. This came out clearly in their first lesson on *kashrus*.

"Not only must meat be from a kosher animal, but the animal must be slaughtered properly, and then the meat has to be *kashered*." As the rabbi said this, he noticed the boy looking very agitated.

"What about fish?" Anthony asked.

"Fish do not have to be killed in a certain way, or *kashered* afterwards. To be considered kosher, a fish must have fins and scales."

"That should be easier," said Anthony. "I thought I would have to tell my stepmother I was becoming a vegetarian. Now I will just say I don't eat meat."

The rabbi fell silent, suddenly aware that this was probably the first time a *bar-mitzvah* boy was taking him seriously.

"Perhaps I should ask my father and stepmother," said Anthony. "They could just buy *kashered* meat."

"Ask them, of course," said the rabbi, "but it is far more than that." He took a booklet on *kashrus* from his drawer.

"Please, read this," Rabbi Levy said. "We will then discuss the first part tomorrow."

Anthony was progressing well with his Hebrew reading, to Yaakov's surprise and delight.

However, on the home front, Anthony encountered complications.

"Aunt Sheila?" (They had agreed that this was what Anthony should call his stepmother). "Aunt Sheila, the rabbi gave me a book about keeping a kosher home. Do you think we can keep a kosher home over here?"

"Absolutely not!" she said, still quite pleasantly. "None of our friends do that."

"But a Jew can't eat *treif* meat," said Anthony.

Sheila Isaacson took the book from Anthony's hands.

"Oh, don't worry Anthony, you just have to learn this for your *bar-mitzvah*. It is part of the syllabus. You don't have to actually keep it. You just have to know it. You have to know all the little laws and rules. No one expects you to keep it. I am sure the rabbi doesn't expect you to. He has to, at least publicly, as he could lose his job, but we are just ordinary, clean living, moral people who don't steal or murder. We don't have to do all that."

"But we do," insisted Anthony. "It is for everyone."

"Don't let the rabbi put funny ideas into your head about that, Anthony. All we asked him to do was to teach you what you have to know for your *bar-mitzvah.*" Her voice was beginning to sound irritated. "He knows no one takes it practically nowadays. He would be very surprised if you kept any of it. He doesn't expect you to. No one expects you to."

Anthony frowned. "What if you are supposed to? Would you do it then?" asked Anthony.

"Absolutely not," she said. "I am not going to let some rabbi tell me my kitchen is not clean. Go and look at it. It's spotless!"

"Would you mind if I eat fish and not meat?" asked Anthony.

"You will eat what is served to you!" said Sheila, getting angry. "You love roast chicken and potatoes baked in the chicken fat. Are you going to tell me that you don't want to eat that? We have mince casserole tonight, your favorite. Forget about it. I mean, learn what you are required to, but don't let it influence your actions at all."

Rabbi Levy quickly realized that he was, in this instance, going to call down the wrath of Ari's parents, but this young man was a Jew, soon to be *bar-mitzvah*, responsible for all six hundred and thirteen commandments. He appeared to be willing and eager to keep them, and the rabbi decided that the only thing he could do was to teach him everything he could. There was no way he could hold it back from him. He hoped they would not take Ari away to someone else, but he felt he just had no option, nor in fact did he want any option. Ari's enthusiasm about everything he learned was indeed an inspiration. Particularly challenging were Ari's deep and searching questions. He was not one to follow things blindly.

Ari began to spend more and more time after his learning sessions with Yaakov. The two boys were becoming firm friends.

"Anthony, do you have to spend so much time on your Hebrew homework?"

Mr. Isaacson was worried. His wife had confided to him her fears about his son's over-involvement, to the point that he wanted to eat kosher food, and Mr. Isaacson felt he should do something about it. He, too, was beginning to notice Anthony's refusal to eat any kind of meat in the house. It wasn't healthy for a young boy! It was abnormal!

"I have a lot to catch up," Anthony answered his father. "My *bar-mitzvah* is not far off."

"I didn't work so hard for it," Mr. Isaacson said. "My boy, you are taking it too seriously. What about your schoolwork? Surely you are neglecting it!"

Anthony opened his school case and showed him several exercise books, opening them to show him his latest marks.

"Hey, son! Anthony! You are clever! All these marks are in the eighties. You are doing very well. I can see the teachers are very pleased with you." He pointed to the 'excellent' stamps on several of the tests.

"I can cope with both, Dad," he said. "And I do my homework."

"What about sports?" asked his father.

"I am going to join the athletics team," said Anthony. "I train every day for it."

"By yourself?" asked his father.

"No, with my friend," said Anthony, for some reason not mentioning that his friend was, in fact, Yaakov. "We run for several miles all around the area."

His father nodded in approval. He was glad his son was looking happier, and the *bar-mitzvah* would soon be here, and the *bar-mitzvah* lessons over. He supposed some boys were influenced by what they were learning, and Anthony had been through a terrible time only very recently. He would get over it. What was a brief flash of inspiration? Even he had had it once, for a few seconds, also at his *bar-mitzvah* time. On his thirteenth Hebrew birthday, he had put on *tefillin* for the first (and of course the last) time. He had felt a stirring inside of himself just for those few minutes. But this had not seriously influenced him. The boy would forget about it, too.

"We have to discuss what you would like for your *bar-mitzvah* present," said his father. "We were thinking about a 50cc motor bike."

"That's great. But, actually, I'd really like a set of *tefillin*, Dad."

"*Tefillin*? That's a waste of money! You put them on only once, and that's that. We can borrow some for you. In fact, I think a friend of mine's son got his own *tefillin* for his *bar-mitzvah*. Goodness knows what for. He's married now and has a son who is nearly eight. He will be able to use them for his *bar-mitzvah*. But he could lend them to us, I am sure, just for one day. I suppose it is good to keep as a memento of the *bar-mitzvah*. But we'd like to get you something practical, something you will use every day."

"I would use them every day," said Anthony.

"Now, Anthony," said his father. "Don't make us worry about you. No one does that any more. It went out with the last century! This is the modern age, the age of computers and fax machines. I am sure it isn't even easy nowadays to buy *tefillin*. I mean, where do you get them? I haven't seen them in the shops."

"The rabbi wanted to get them for me," said Anthony.

His father was thoughtful, but he didn't really see that Anthony was serious.

"Well, maybe we will just give you a gift of money, and you can spend it as you want. I wouldn't waste it on *tefillin* if I were you. How much are they, anyway? There are far more useful and interesting things you can buy."

Sheila was right, thought Mr. Isaacson. Anthony was becoming over-influenced. Thank goodness it would soon be over.

SEVEN

"Yes, I am going to be sleeping there," said Anthony. "That's what the rabbi said."

"It is really not necessary," said Sheila Isaacson. "You can learn about the Sabbath from a book. You can go on Friday night, and I will fetch you in the car."

Anthony blushed.

"No, Aunt Sheila," he said. "You can't drive on *Shabbos*. They want me to stay there the whole *Shabbos*. Dad can pick me up on Saturday night."

"I will speak to your father," she said. Perhaps it would be a good idea to let him go for a full *Shabbos*. It would show him how restrictive and narrow religious Judaism was. Years ago, one of her friends had gone to a *Shabbaton*. She had not even been allowed to switch on her "Walkman." Perhaps it would make him see that his rosy picture of Judaism had many, many thorns. Perhaps it would cure him.

With this hope in mind, Anthony's parents allowed him to pack a small suitcase and spend *Shabbos* with the rabbi and his family. Both his father and his stepmother had told him that he would be in for a very difficult time, and that long before it was finished he would be phoning them to come and fetch him, if he did not in fact repack his case and walk home.

"These people live in the Dark Ages," said his father. "They have nothing in common with us. You will have hours and hours of undiluted religion. It will be terrible." He wrinkled his nose up at the thought. "It must be really terrible to be trapped like that for a whole twenty-four hours. I want you to go and see how much you hate it." He laughed, confident of what he was saying.

As soon as Anthony entered the Levy's house just before *Shabbos* began, he felt as if he had stepped into another world. He had read about *Shabbos,* and was already becoming familiar with all its laws, and he was in the rabbi's home several days a week, but he had expected nothing like this.

The house itself seemed to glow with *Shabbos,* and when Sara Levy lit the candles, the glow seemed to penetrate into his very soul.

He had actually never watched a woman kindle the *Shabbos* lights. It moved him far beyond what he could express. He also felt a deep sense of belonging, not only in the rabbi's home, but even of belonging, as it were, to *Shabbos,* as if the spirit of *Shabbos* enveloped him and brought him into a new dimension.

He saw that the dining room table, covered with a gleaming white cloth, had been extended to almost double its size. Would there be other guests besides himself?

When they returned from *shul,* Rabbi Levy brought several guests with him. Anthony felt he could finally merge his two worlds: the Ari and the Anthony. Not one of the other guests was *frum*. They were people like his father and stepmother, commenting on the oddities and the quaintness of Jewish life, and looking at the rabbi blankly as he spoke about the practical aspects of Judaism.

Anthony now knew that Judaism and Jewish practice was not only for rabbis and their families. Judaism was for every Jew. He could not understand why most people thought it wasn't. Couldn't they see how its learning and its practice satisfied on so many levels? Couldn't they see how exciting it was to learn each new concept and the discussions around it? How could they live, ignoring so much of what seemed to him to be life itself?

The rabbi had discussed with his wife the strength of Ari's attachment both to their family and to *Yiddishkeit*. Sara had expressed the concern that perhaps he was doing all this to please them, just to be accepted by them, which to an extent he was, under any circumstances. But the rabbi had quickly countered that. He sensed that Ari's excitement about Judaism went far beyond his attachment to the Levy family.

Anthony was fetched by his father shortly after *havdalah*, feeling as if he had been in another world, in another dimension.

His father read the inspiration on his face with a certain amount of disgust.

"Don't tell me you enjoyed it," said Mr. Isaacson.

"It was wonderful," Anthony said. "I am going there next week, too," he added.

His father suddenly became angry as he jolted the car to a halt and went to open the garage gates.

"You most certainly will not go there again next week!" he shouted. "This is not part of the *bar-mitzvah* syllabus. I went to that rabbi, trusting him to teach you what you needed to know, trusting him to respect the family you came from, and he rides rough-shod over all of us and tries to influence you! How dare he!"

He slammed the car door and opened the front door.

His wife took one look at him and went back to the television program she had been watching. She knew that when her husband was in such a mood, it was best that she say nothing. He marched his son up to his room and closed the door behind him.

"I have to talk to you," he said. "These *bar-mitzvah* lessons have got to stop immediately. I am sure you already know far too much. I will arrange for you to have a few final lessons with a proper Hebrew teacher who doesn't think it's necessary to tell you to act on every fantasy you learn about."

Anthony was dumbstruck.

"The *bar-mitzvah* is quite soon," he said quietly.

"Thank goodness!" said his father. "And then all this will be at an end. But I can't let my son make a public spectacle of himself in the streets, and therefore a spectacle of his family. This is a decent area, and decent people live here."

Anthony frowned, and his father realized he didn't know what he was referring to.

"A colleague of mine, someone who respected me and I hope still does, told me what you were doing along the streets. Disgusting, I call it," Mr. Isaacson said.

Anthony looked more puzzled.

"What did he say?" he asked.

"He told me he had seen you and another boy, obviously the rabbi's son, running through the streets, both with *yarmulkas* on your heads."

Anthony nodded.

"How long have you been doing this?" he demanded.

"We've been running together," said Anthony. "But you knew that."

"I knew you were running with a friend, but I didn't know it was the rabbi's son, and I certainly didn't know you would disgrace and embarrass us in the streets like that. What do you think the neighbors thought when they saw you with that on your head? This isn't Jerusalem. This isn't a synagogue. It is a street. It is *our* neighborhood!"

Anthony said nothing.

Mr. Isaacson took a deep breath. His wife softly entered the room and sat next to him.

"We have decided that you are not to have any contact at all with the Levy family," said Anthony's father. "I made a mistake taking you to them, but I suppose you have learned something. I will make other arrangements for your *bar-mitzvah* immediately. I cannot have their interference any more."

Neither of them were prepared for Anthony's reaction.

He turned a ghastly white and started to speak to them with a calmness and a coolness which made them shiver inwardly a little.

"You don't love me," he said. "Neither of you loves me. You don't really care about me. You only care about the neighbors and what they will say. My mother was right. You, Dad, never, ever cared about me, about us. You found someone else, married her and lived in luxury while you left us to try to find something decent to eat from the money we got from you and from Mum's small salary. You don't care that I was so unhappy when Mum died. I was so lonely until I found real friendship in the Levy family. But because you don't really care, you want to take it away from me."

"But we care," said Sheila.

"You say you care because you have to say that. You try to be nice to me, but only because you have to. The Levys really like me for who I am. And Yaakov is my best friend, the best friend I ever had, much more than Stephen. And now you want to take it away.

"Mum said, Dad, that you treated people like puppets,

pulling the strings you wanted. I didn't believe that, but now I do. You just want to take away what means everything to me."

Both adults had become white. Sheila spoke first.

"That isn't true about your father, and you will learn it isn't true. Your mother taught you to hate us."

"Don't talk about my mother!" said Anthony angrily. "You both hurt her enough."

His face suddenly contorted with pain and he started to cry and cry. Mr. Isaacson stood up.

"I am not to be persuaded otherwise, Anthony. I am speaking to that rabbi tomorrow. It is for your own good, Anthony," he said. "For your future!"

Eight

Anthony hardly spoke the entire week which followed this angry discussion. He did not contact the rabbi, nor run with Yaakov. His stepmother kept an eye out that he would not do that.

However, he continued to refuse to eat meat, and spent hours on his Hebrew and Jewish studies.

"It's a phase. He'll get over it," said his father.

Wednesday night of the following week, the Isaacsons, except for Anthony, who was working in his room, were busy watching television. The two younger children were playing with a toy garage in the center of the room. Mr. Isaacson, who loved dinky cars, had bought Jules at least twenty of them. They were arranging the cars, lining them up, and Debby was counting.

"These cars are one, two, three, four and these cars . . . these cars are *alef, beis* and *gimmel.* But where is *daled?*" said Jules. "You must have *daled.*"

Mr. Isaacson nearly shot out of his seat.

"Who taught you that?" he demanded.

The children looked at him, puzzled.

"Anthony did," they said. "He gave me sweets because I was doing so well," said Debby.

"He gave me some also," said Jules. "He said I had done extra well on this lesson."

Lessons? Was Anthony trying to influence the children? Would they soon have to contend with Jules wanting to go to school in a *yarmulka*?

"When did he give you these lessons?" demanded their mother.

"Oh," said Debby, "on *Shabbos*, when we were playing in his room. He told us stories and all kinds of things, and then taught us *alef-beis*."

On Thursday, things began to change. Rabbi Levy visited Mr. Isaacson in his office. Though Anthony never heard what was actually said, he understood that the two men had a very long conversation.

To his surprise and delight, his father announced to his family that they had all been invited to the Levy's house for a meal on Friday night, and that they were all going to meet them there directly after *shul*. They were not going to *shul*, of course. Even Mrs. Isaacson seemed somehow less resistant, and agreed with her husband that they should accept the invitation. She had not been blind to her stepson's increasing despair, and the separation just seemed to be making things worse. This "religion thing" was just a phase. He needed the rabbi at this time, someone extra to talk to. And as for the rabbi's son, well, Anthony did need a friend in the neighborhood.

The Isaacsons thought that perhaps it would be better to meet the family themselves so as to be able to guide Anthony better. They could see the flaws and the drawbacks more clearly, and point them out to him. After all, he was just a boy, a child, and a very, very hurt child at that. Being basically a good-natured woman, it hurt Sheila to see Anthony so unhappy. Keeping him away from the Levys had not really worked, though she had to agree it might work in the long run. In these circumstances she realized, however, that if she didn't do something she might find herself having to look after an extremely difficult young man.

So it was that on that *Shabbos,* the family actually walked the few blocks to the rabbi's home. There had been a lot of discussion about taking the car and parking around the corner, but when Anthony said that he would then meet them there and Debby insisted that she be allowed to go with him, Mr. Isaacson decided that no harm would be done by walking.

Anthony felt overjoyed to be in the rabbi's house again, and his father and stepmother were both relieved and a little uneasy to see the way he relaxed and seemed to sparkle in the Levy's home.

Despite their antagonism about the way Anthony was being influenced, the Isaacsons could not help liking Rabbi and Mrs. Levy, as well as Yaakov and the other children.

Sheila Isaacson looked carefully at Yaakov's elder sisters, Rochel and Nechama, as they helped their mother serve the meal. She could not help feeling that perhaps this was how she would like her own daughter to grow up, instead of being part of the disco-club scene like so many of her friends' daughters.

But she soon put this out of her mind.

There was another family, also, at the *Shabbos* table, Dr. and Mrs. Eisenberg and their eight-year-old son. They were obviously not religious in the slightest way, and in fact, as they confided to Mr. Isaacson, they had parked their car around the corner. The latter had felt good that at least he had an ally in his non-observance. After all, religion was for rabbis, not for the general public.

But despite his antagonism, Mr. Isaacson, and indeed the doctor, could not help but be entranced by the rabbi's storytelling, during which time the children would appear as if from nowhere and gather at the table to listen. Even Debby, quite forgetting that this was the first time she had met a rabbi, immediately asked, "Tell us another one."

The food, of course, was delicious. In fact, except for the few formal occasions when the Isaacsons had eaten in hotels, they had not sat down to a meal with so many courses. They, too, began to feel at home, and began to feel that perhaps religion wasn't so bad after all.

During the walk home, however, after the spell of the *Shabbos* table had worn off a little, their antagonism returned.

Jules was crying to be picked up. When Anthony had whispered to him that it was better for his father not to carry him on *Shabbos,* Mr. Isaacson became angry. He whisked the protesting Jules onto his shoulders and turned on Anthony.

"You should be grateful we visited your rabbi," he said. "We did that for you. But your rabbi never told us what to do except to say initially that he would prefer it if we didn't come by car. But he didn't even say we couldn't. He just said he would 'prefer' it. You are being more religious than the rabbi. You are telling us what to do."

Anthony was silent. He had been so happy that evening, and his family seemed to have enjoyed themselves. Now it seemed it was turning in an unpleasant direction. Was he now going to be banned from the house again? He let out a deep sigh.

His stepmother intervened.

"We liked the Levys very much," she said. "But they are

from a different world, a completely different world. We have nothing, really, in common with them. Neither do the people in their congregation! Didn't you see the cars driving away from the synagogue when we arrived? I'm sure the rabbi made it clear that he didn't want them to drive on *Shabbos*, but they knew that they didn't have to take him seriously. It is like that everywhere. I think on the Day of Atonement at the Great Synagogue, someone even got knocked down by a car in the parking lot, the traffic was so congested.

"And do you think that coming by car affected everyone's fasting or affected their ability to listen to the beautiful operatic singing of the cantor?"

Mr. Isaacson nodded as Sheila spoke. He seemed to calm down somewhat.

"Anthony, son, I know you like these people. They are very warm, nice people, and I can see that Yaakov, even though he keeps all these odd customs, is basically a bright young man. I can see why you would be friends with him. But such things don't last. Their world was drowned in the ocean somewhere between Lithuania and South Africa around the turn of the century. Your great grandparents, Anthony, were part of that world. In fact if I am not mistaken, we even had a rabbi or two way, way back. But nobody keeps these things now. It isn't socially acceptable or practical. Please don't make a mockery of our family. I don't want the world to see my son as odd."

Anthony flinched. The old depression was returning, but was displaced immediately by his father's next words.

"I had a long, long talk with the rabbi," Mr. Isaacson went on. "We decided that you should still learn with him and still have contact with the family . . ."

He suddenly received a bear hug from Anthony which caused Jules, who was asleep on his father's shoulders, to wake up with a loud protest and almost kick him. Everyone burst out laughing.

"A pity I don't have my camera," said Sheila, laughing. "You should have just seen what you looked like then with your two sons wrapped around you."

Anthony looked at her. No, she wasn't so bad, as stepmothers go. Perhaps one day he could even really like her.

"But," his father added, when everything seemed to have calmed down, "but, we discussed at length your involvement in this. The rabbi insists that he is not pushing you, he is just teaching you what you should know. He said it is you, or something inside of you, a *nishmo*, or something he said, a sort of soul. I don't understand all of that and I don't want to."

His voice had an accusing ring.

NINE

It was a week before the *bar-mitzvah*, and Anthony wanted to visit his mother's grave. After discussing it with the rabbi, he broached the subject with his father. Rabbi Levy said that he often had occasion informally to visit the cemetery, and that he would take Anthony there, but he wanted him to ask his father's permission first.

Mr. Isaacson looked uncomfortable.

"Are you sure you need to go, Anthony?" he asked, knowing that if the boy wanted to, he most definitely should, but at the same time wanting to blot out the prospect of an unpleasant emotional experience.

"Yes, Dad. I really want to. It will be my *bar-mitzvah* soon, and I want to visit Mum before then," he had said.

At the words "visit Mum," Mr. Isaacson flushed. Didn't the child know that his mother had been dead almost a year already?

He no longer wanted to think about it.

"I don't want you to upset yourself, son," he said. "You are just getting over it."

He didn't tell his father that the loss of his mother was still a persistent, nagging pain which sometimes got better and at other times overcame him. How could his father know of the many times he had cried himself to sleep?

"The rabbi goes to the cemetery sometimes," he said. "Maybe I could ask him if I could go with him."

As long as Mr. Isaacson didn't have to participate, he didn't see any real harm in allowing the boy to go. A Sunday did not have to be spoiled on account of his ex-wife.

"Please ask him, Anthony. If he is going already, I am sure he will take you."

It felt strange to be in the cemetery, a cemetery that looked very different without the rain and the mud and the people milling around. It was quiet and peaceful, with rows and rows of graves.

Anthony read the inscription on his mother's headstone.

Strange, the inscription read as if from him, her son, Anthony, and yet he did not remember having had anything to do with it. Why hadn't his father asked him? Perhaps he thought it would have upset him too much.

He felt strange, standing at his mother's grave, as if time had stood still. Had it, for her?

After seeing that Anthony was all right, the rabbi had gone to the main building to sort out something for one of his congregants.

There did not seem to be anyone around except for an older couple standing in front of a grave at some distance. If he wanted to speak to his mother, he would have to do so now. But could he do so? Maybe one didn't *do* these things? Perhaps he would be talking to himself.

But then, into his mind came the picture of the box being lowered and the sound of the mud being shovelled onto it, and hot tears began to flow down his cheeks.

"Mum . . ." he said. "Mum, I don't know if you can hear me, but I don't know where else to find you, and I want to talk to you."

He dried his tears and blew his nose hard, but the tears continued to run as though he had unleashed a mountain spring. Would they never stop?

"Mum, it is going to be my *bar-mitzvah* soon. Remember? I so wanted you to be at my *bar-mitzvah*. Remember how we talked about it?"

He collapsed onto the ground next to the grave and wept and wept. Eventually he stood up. There was something he had to say.

"Mum, we didn't know what it means to be *bar-mitzvah*. We didn't know that it means that I now accept upon myself to keep all the *mitzvos*. We didn't even know anything, really, about what the *mitzvos* are. But you are in heaven now, Mum, in what the rabbi calls the World of Truth. So you know what is truly important in this world, and what is not. And you know, now, that this is an upside down world where unimportant things are made to be of extreme importance.

"Now you know that Torah and *mitzvos* are the only things of real value, that that's the reason why we are on earth, often having such difficulties.

"Even though Dad and Aunt Sheila can't understand it, as soon as I am *bar-mitzvah*, I am going to be *frum*. I am going to keep everything. I am going to wear a *yarmulka* and *tzitzis*, even to school. I am going to keep *Shabbos* and *Yom Tov*. I am going to use my *bar-mitzvah* money for *tefillin* and for a kosher *mezuzah* for my room.

"And Mum," he said, tears still running down his cheeks, "I will never, ever eat *treif* again. I will spend my pocket money on *matzoh* and kosher tuna and fruit and *parve* sweets, and I will never eat at home again until it is kosher over there. And if, perhaps, I really get hungry, I can eat something at the rabbi's home. Mum, I know quite a lot of Hebrew already, and I have been learning with Yaakov, my best friend. I have been learning all kinds of things with Yaakov, and it's so exciting, much more exciting than at school.

"Oh Mum, talking of school, you are going to be very pleased with me. I am getting a prize because I have come in at the top of my class. Even my math has become quite good. Aunt Sheila isn't so bad. I know she hurt you a lot, but maybe it doesn't hurt any more where you are. Aunt Sheila helps me with algebra; that is why I am doing so well in it.

"One day, Mum, I will have my own home, and there will be *mezuzos* on all the doors and on *Shabbos* it will be really *Shabbos* and it will be really, really kosher. Oh Mum, oh Mum, if only you could visit me in it! But Mum, you are not even able to come to my *bar-mitzvah*!"

He leaned on the headstone, crying. Suddenly he was aware of a strong arm around him.

It was the rabbi, who had stood silently for several minutes listening to Anthony speaking out his heart to his mother.

"You have a special *neshamah*, Ari," he said. "A very, very special *neshamah*."

Anthony was still looking shocked and strained when they arrived back home. The rabbi took him inside. He greeted the family and took Anthony up to his room.

"It was too much for him," said Mr. Isaacson, looking anxiously at the rabbi when he emerged from Anthony's room.

"It was something that needed to be done," said the rabbi. "I think this experience gets something out of a person's system."

"But he was beginning to forget," said his father.

"People don't forget so quickly," said the rabbi. "They just don't talk so much about it, and other people forget, so they feel the person should be over it already. With the initial shock of losing a person close to you, the person who is left has a natural anaesthetic. As this wears off over the months, the person feels their loss more and more, but by this time, they can't talk to anyone about it, because people look at them in surprise and say, 'Why now? You took it so bravely and so well! Why now, after all this time?'"

Mr. Isaacson nodded.

"How is he doing with his *bar-mitzvah* studies?" he asked.

"Very well, extremely well," he said. "Your son has a very special soul. He has taken to learning with an enthusiasm I have seldom seen."

"I am sure you will miss your student when it is all over next week," said Mr. Isaacson. "In six months you really gave him a comprehensive Jewish education."

"But this is only the beginning," said the rabbi.

"No, wait a minute," Mr. Isaacson said, suddenly flushing with anger. "No one learns past their *bar-mitzvah*. This is a sort of graduation. He doesn't need any more of this. What else is there to learn? He seems to know everything already."

Feeling that this was not really the time to go into this, Rabbi Levy left. From what he had heard Ari say at the graveside, he knew he was about to face a great deal of family opposition. He sighed. On the other hand, perhaps he should be more optimistic. Opposition, in the long run, would only strengthen him!

TEN

No one could say that the *bar-mitzvah* wasn't impressive. No one could deny that Anthony read in a clear, confident voice which could not help but make his parents proud of him.

All the Isaacson's friends who came to the synagogue for the occasion were suitably impressed, and after the ceremony, they smothered them in praises and delighted comments about their brilliant son from Durban.

They looked forward to the *bar-mitzvah* reception, booked in one of the next suburb's halls for that evening.

Jules and Debby were bursting with pride. They left their parents' sides in *shul* to sit with the rabbi's children. Jules sat with Yaakov's younger brother, Zevi, and Debby with Miriam, the girl in the family nearest her age.

The Levy children, too, who had come to know Ari well, were very proud of him.

They all looked forward to the evening party. Since it was a *bar-mitzvah* affair, the Isaacsons had readily agreed to strictly kosher catering. After all, this was the accepted practice, even in their social circles.

The party, in fact, was going without a hitch. The food was served tastefully and efficiently. Presents, mostly of checks, came forth in abundance from all the guests. The band played well, and the atmosphere was stylish and pleasant. Who could ask for more? Anthony's father was very comfortable and pleased with himself.

But then it was time for Anthony to speak.

The boy took his place at the center with a certain authority and started a *pilpul* which he and the rabbi and Yaakov had worked on. Most of the guests looked totally blank, at the same time having to admit that Anthony spoke forcefully and well.

But at his next remarks, his father and stepmother became extremely anxious. Several of their friends raised their eyebrows and exchanged glances.

Anthony explained that a *bar-mitzvah* was a time in a person's life when he becomes answerable on his own to Hashem for all the *mitzvos*. He proclaimed that he had now taken upon himself to do everything, no matter at what cost. He said that for centuries, Jews had faced death rather than give up their adherence to *mitzvos*, and that they had died because they had something worth dying for.

He also said that up to now, he had been known as Anthony, but that now he would use his Hebrew name which he was given at his *bris*, Aryeh, or Ari for short.

After this, he expressed his gratitude to his mother, to his father and stepmother for giving him a home, and especially to Aunt Sheila who had helped him with his math.

He gave a special message to his half brother and sister, who nearly burst with pride when he mentioned their names.

He then thanked the rabbi and his family, and Yaakov for being his friend, teacher, *chavrusa* and running partner.

When he sat down after proposing a toast to his family, people applauded, but then sank into a somewhat stunned silence. The boy had spoken very well, but obviously he didn't really mean what he said. A *bar-mitzvah* might have meant that years ago, but in today's world, it was completely different.

The Isaacsons were dumbfounded by Anthony's speech. How could he be totally *frum*? They certainly weren't going to change around their kitchen or their shopping lists or their home for him. Surely he couldn't expect it of them! After some thought, however, Mr. Isaacson dismissed Anthony's speech. Obviously the rabbi had written it for him. It was just the rabbi's style for a *bar-mitzvah* speech.

Mrs. Isaacson, however, was more anxious about it. Being at home all the time, she had more contact with Anthony, and she knew it was quite possible that the boy meant every word. She also knew it was very possible that it was Anthony, and not the rabbi, who had added to his speech.

She also had further anxieties at the *bar-mitzvah* ceremony and at the reception. Both her younger children appeared to have become extremely friendly with the rabbi's children. She would definitely try to keep out any of that influence from her home.

As the music played, and as the guests flocked around Anthony and his parents, Mr. Isaacson explained to his friends, especially his colleagues at work, that the rabbi had written every word of the boy's speech.

Some of his friends, however, expressed admiration for the boy's courage.

"You'll have a rabbi for a son," several people said.

"Such a clever young man," others said.

But Anthony's father refused to believe that they could be sincere. He had to dispel any illusions they had about his son being religious.

Back at home, after the *bar-mitzvah*, the atmosphere was tense. Mr. Isaacson told his son that he had done very well in his speech until he had chosen to shame them publicly by announcing his odd ideas. What would his colleagues be saying? Did he hate them so much that he had to say those things? Didn't he know how much it would hurt them?

Anthony felt very alone.

"I meant what I said," he said, "every word of it. And I know that you are always worried about what your friends and neighbors and people at work would say, so I told them all at once, so that you won't worry any more. They will all be used to it. They won't say, 'Look at what Mr. Isaacson's son is doing,' because I have already told them what I am doing, and you don't have to explain anything to them."

Mr. Isaacson decided to drop the subject temporarily.

"Shall we open some of the envelopes and see what is inside?" he asked. "And also all these presents."

Jules and Debby, who had been on their way to bed, exhausted from the evening out, were suddenly wide awake.

Twenty minutes later, the presents had amounted to ten books, three *Kiddush* cups, two Personal Organizer files, one camera and five photograph albums.

He had 300 rand in book tokens and 1560 rand in cash.

"We will make that 2560 rand," said his father, handing him an envelope. "I suppose it is going to be *tefillin,* but you are going to have quite a bit left over."

Anthony hugged his father.

"Dad, one day you will be proud of me, really proud of me!"

"Well, at the rate you are doing at school, I am proud of you already. I hope I am looking at a future civil engineer."

Anthony smiled. He did not want to tell him that bridges and stresses and strains of buildings did not interest him in the slightest, and that he could never in a thousand years see himself in front of a drawing board. This was not the time to tell him that. Now he had his *tefillin* secured, his *mezuzah*, a hot-plate to cook on upstairs in his room, and even a bike. The holidays were coming up, and he and Yaakov had planned all kinds of excursions for the two weeks in which their holidays overlapped.

He knew he would face conflict and difficulty, but for now, he would enjoy the momentary peace for as long as it lasted.

Eleven

"We can leave our bikes at the Suikerbossie Restaurant parking area," said Ari. "I checked with my geography teacher when he gave me the map. Then we can start the walk."

Yaakov and Ari turned off the main coastal road between Llandudno and Hout Bay, and followed the signboard to the restaurant.

They had left early, straight after *davening*, to follow the Suikerbossie (Sugar Bush) Circuit Trail.

Leaving their bikes as planned, after carefully locking them to an adjacent pole, they followed the fence around the underground reservoir and walked along the avenue of pines towards the wide fire-break near the top of the well. They followed more lines of pines until they could see Hout Bay looking almost like a Swiss lake between the mountains.

"We should be at the waterfall in about an hour," said Yaakov. "That is, according to your map."

He ran his finger along towards Myburgh's Waterfall ravine.

"We go from there up the mountain. It's about fifteen minutes of climbing up the left bank. Then we can rest and eat something and learn a bit."

Ari had been told not to follow the path into the ravine but rather to look for the path on the edge of the forest going sharply to the left. There they would begin the climb.

They reached the waterfall and drank thirstily from their water bottles. From their running practice, both boys were fairly fit, but the climb had made them tired, and it took them some time to regain their energy.

As they followed the river bed dwarfed by the majestic Yellowood trees, they were struck by the sheer beauty of the place. They were surrounded by hundreds of red disas flowers. Water trickled from the moss in tiny rivulets.

"Yaakov," said Ari, as they paused to admire the beauty around them. "Yaakov, tell me more about your school. I know it's a *yeshivah*, but you learn all the ordinary school subjects, too, don't you?"

"Yes, we do," said Yaakov. "That's why I come home from school such a long time after you. We have a double syllabus—Hebrew in the morning and secular in the afternoon."

Was Ari thinking of coming to his school? Was there any chance that his father would agree to it?

"What time will you come home this year?" Ari asked.

"Four o'clock on some days, but later on others. There is school on three Sundays of every month," said Yaakov.

"Do you think I would be able to catch up with the class if I were to come to your school?"

"You would have to go into the *mechinah* class at first," he said. "They have special teachers there to help you catch up in your Hebrew studies. I would love to have you with me in the school."

Ari was becoming more and more interested.

"But there is one problem," said Yaakov, a little embarrassed. "The school you go to now is a good one, but it is almost free. You have to pay school fees for the *yeshivah*, otherwise the teacher could not get paid and the school couldn't survive. Would your father pay for a school like that?"

"You know, Yaakov," said Ari, "if you had asked that a few days ago, I would have agreed that it was in no way possible. My father had a visitor, a lawyer connected with my mother's firm of lawyers in Durban. She left me money, I think quite a lot of money, and I never even knew she had that much money. She was saving it for my education. There was a clause in her will that if she should die while I was still a minor, my father and the lawyers would be the trustees. But if I were to need the money for education, especially with a view to my future, I could apply for it."

"I doubt if she was talking about a *yeshivah*," said Yaakov. "I mean, she wasn't religious at all, was she?"

"No, not all. She probably meant it for extra math lessons, or perhaps for me to go to a boarding school if things got too tough with my father. But the way it is worded, the money could be used for *yeshivah*." He began to get more and more excited.

"But what about your father?" asked Yaakov.

"I will ask him," said Ari. "Oh, if only he will say yes."

They continued on their way, pausing to look at the magnificent view over the treetops in the Orange Kloof of the Cape Flats, and False Bay through the gap of Constantia Nek.

Even Yaakov was amazed.

"Do you know what?" he said. "I've lived in Cape Town all my life, and I have been up Table Mountain in the cable car, but I have never seen a view like this!"

It was late as they made their way home, and they

eventually arrived quite exhausted. Yaakov had to be at *shul* in time for *Minchah.* Ari *davened* with him, and then made for home at top speed. One day he would be able to attend the rabbi's *shiur* between *Minchah* and *Maariv,* but not yet. Even though he had been true to his word and was keeping every *mitzvah* he knew about, his father still kept a tight rein on his activities.

Ari was having many of his own sessions with Yaakov and the rabbi. Contrary to what his father had imagined a *bar-mitzvah* graduation to be, his learning had increased considerably. It had been only the beginning.

"That's what I want you to do, something healthy. Not spending all your time on religion. That is how I like my son to look, exhausted but happy from a bit of climbing."

Mr. Isaacson looked at him with approval. "I know that walk you did," he said. "It is one of the tougher ones. You have to be pretty fit for it."

Ari sank heavily into a chair. It had been tough, but very, very good.

"You are going again these holidays, I hope. Which walk are you going to do this time?"

"We are going to explore some caves," said Ari. "There are a lot around Muizenberg and Kalk Bay. The mountains are riddled with them. Apparently there are more than sixty in all. Yaakov is getting a detailed guide from the Parks and Forest branch of the Cape Town City Council."

"That sounds really exciting," said his father. "Besides your running, it's good practice for making the athletics team."

"Dad," said Ari, "I'm not going to be able to make the athletics team, at least, not in my school." Could this be the opening he was watching for?

"Why ever not?" asked Mr. Isaacson. "Anthony, don't underestimate yourself. Of course you will make it. I have seen myself that your standards are high."

"It's not that, Dad," said Ari. "In fact, as far as that goes, they already asked me to be in the team."

"They asked you?" asked his father, amazed that his son hadn't told them. "But what is the problem, then?"

"I told them I could not be in the team, Dad. A lot of what they do is on *Shabbos*." He knew there would be a strong reaction from his father and he became a little uneasy as he saw him flush with anger.

"It's going too far," he said. "Your religion is going to stifle you and take away everything that is good in life."

"That is because it isn't a Jewish school," said Ari. "If it had been a Jewish school, they wouldn't have done anything on *Shabbos*. I would have been able to go into the team."

His father's color changed from red to white.

"So that is what you are after! You are being sly with me. You want me to send you to Yaakov's school. You want to spend the whole day studying religion, not getting a metric, having to live on charity!"

Sheila walked into the room, looking somewhat alarmed. It wasn't often that she heard her husband shouting like that. He turned to her immediately.

"He wants to go and be a rabbi and forget about his education," he said.

"It isn't that," said Ari. "But it is true, I would like to go to Yaakov's school. They have a double program there, general secular education and Jewish education. You can get a metric there, and you can go straight from there to university."

"With school hours as they are, you won't have much time for both. Obviously your secular education suffers if you are taught by a bunch of fanatical rabbis!" shouted his father.

"The hours are much longer, Dad," said Ari quietly. "Sometimes I will come home at four in the afternoon. Sometimes I won't be home until after six, and I would have only one Sunday free in a month. And we start earlier because of *davening*."

His stepmother suddenly became very thoughtful, but her husband didn't notice this.

"And you talk of an athletics team," said his father. "You will turn into one of those miserable weaklings who never sees sunlight. I can just imagine it!"

"Dad," Ari went on, "there are school fees to pay. But didn't the lawyer say that my mother had left money for educational purposes?"

"That interfering woman!" shouted his father. "Her hand reaches from the grave to help her son disobey my wishes!"

"Please Anthony, go up to your room," said Aunt Sheila. "Your father and I will discuss it. You are upsetting him. You won't get anywhere with this now. Please leave it alone for a while."

Ari went to his room and shut the door. His heart was pounding and his hands were clammy and wet. He had known there would be a fight about his attending the *yeshivah*, but it was a fight he hoped he would somehow win.

What his father had said about his mother had shocked him. He had never ever spoken against her to him before, and yet, remembering her antagonism to him, there must have been some anger on his part as well. And yet, what he had said gave him an odd comfort. Perhaps his mother's hand had somehow reached beyond the grave to help him.

He wondered what was going on downstairs.

"David, don't shout so much at the boy. He is still so sensitive. Let's discuss it quietly."

Mr. Isaacson looked at his wife. He was still shaking from the encounter.

"I can't have my son making a fool of all of us," he said. "He walks the streets with a *yarmulka* and with those strings sticking out from under his shirt, making a spectacle of himself. He refuses to eat when we visit friends. He won't come out with us on a Saturday. There are all kinds of quite normal things he won't do. He won't eat anything you cook. He is constantly hanging around the rabbi and the rabbi's family. His only friend is Yaakov, who dresses in the same ridiculous way he does. I just can't take it!" The anger was abating, making his voice flat and bitter.

"I also have something to say," said Sheila. "I want to add that I realize, being a stepmother, that I have to tread carefully. I like Anthony, I really do. I like him a lot. But he is beginning to influence Debby and Jules. They are beginning to say the *alef beis* all over the place. Debby asked when we are going to put a *mezuzah* on the front door. Jules even started wearing a cap the other day, saying that Ari, not Anthony, always wears one, so why shouldn't he? I am very, very worried about the influence he is having on them. Soon no one will eat in this house!"

Again Mr. Isaacson turned white.

"He is my son," he said. "He lives here. This is his home. He can't go anywhere else. You can't be asking me to send him away."

"No, no, of course I wouldn't ever suggest that," she said quickly. "But this school he is talking about. The hours are much longer. He is away most Friday night and Saturdays, and goes to school on Sundays. He won't have time to spend with Debby and Jules. He will be living here quite happily, but he will lose most of his influence on the children."

There was dead silence for the next couple of minutes.

Eventually, Mr. Isaacson responded.

"You are right. I will check with the lawyer tomorrow. If everything can be arranged financially, I will phone Rabbi Levy and make arrangements."

TWELVE

Yaakov and Ari were together at the Yeshivah High School for several years. The two of them did almost everything together, and though Ari had made many good friends in the school, it just wasn't the same as having Yaakov constantly around.

Both boys grew and matured, and made great strides in their Hebrew studies.

It took Ari almost two years to catch up completely to his class level, but he eventually began to outstrip his classmates in the depth and content of his learning, at the same time excelling, as Yaakov did, in his secular studies.

Both boys represented the school in the athletics team and did very well.

Yaakov's metric results were so good that he was offered a scholarship to both Cape Town and Rhodes Universities. But of course, he declined. There had never been a question in his mind that he would go anywhere but to a full time *yeshivah.*

Yaakov, being a year ahead of Ari, matriculated and went

straight to the *yeshivah gedolah* of Johannesburg. Ari felt his loss very keenly.

"Ari, you are coming to the Johannesburg Yeshivah next year, aren't you? Have you arranged it with your parents yet? I miss our learning sessions together, you know. Now that you've finished metric, you'll have to come and join me. It's been a whole year!"

Ari's results would be out soon, and he knew, also, that he had done extremely well. At times he half wished he hadn't.

"Yaakov, of course I'm coming to the Johannesburg Yeshivah," said Ari, laughing. "It just takes a bit of time to get my parents used to the idea. I'm coming back with you in January as soon as the new semester starts."

"You haven't spoken to them at all?" asked Yaakov, a little anxiously.

"I will, don't worry," said Ari. "I got to Yeshivah High School, didn't I?"

"Yes, but as you said, your father was always talking about varsity."

"Maybe I won't get a university entrance," said Ari hopefully. "That Physics paper wasn't so good, and I left out a question for fifteen points."

"That was fifteen out of six hundred," said Yaakov. "You haven't a hope of not getting into a university. You will probably also be offered a couple of scholarships, and then what would your father say? My father told me that he met your father in town a few weeks ago. Your father told him what high hopes he had for you in the field of civil or mechanical engineering or architecture."

"Of all the subjects to choose," said Ari. "Even if I weren't *frum*, I wouldn't go into those fields. I would go into medicine or psychology or something. But I don't want to go to varsity.

Ever since my *bar-mitzvah*, I have known that I wanted to go to *yeshivah*."

"I know that," said Yaakov. "Actually, I'm trying to say something else to you, and maybe your mentioning psychology makes it a bit easier."

He paused, a little embarrassed.

"Your father told my father that he's going to send you to a psychologist, a counselling psychologist."

"What on earth for?" asked Ari, somewhat alarmed.

"Well, for one thing, to give you some test as to what kind of direction you should study, but also to see if you are all right."

"You mean, to see if I am normal or not?" asked Ari, aghast.

"Sort of," said Yaakov. "He told my father he thought you had an over-attachment to religion which was not allowing you to achieve in the way you should, and he thought you might have been affected by your mother's death."

Ari suddenly burst out laughing. "I don't believe it!" he said. "My father thinks I'm nuts!"

"Well, just say you won't go," said Yaakov.

"No, I'll go if he wants me to. I know I am not nuts. Of course I'm affected by my mother's death. Anyone would be. But that isn't the reason for my being *frum*," he said. "Maybe if I can convince the psychologist that I am quite normal and that I need to go to *yeshivah*, it might be a good way to tell him."

"Do you think the psychologist would buy that?" asked Yaakov, doubtfully.

"Well, it's worth a try. If they do tests on me to find out about my inner thoughts and wishes, all they are going to find is my attachment to *Yiddishkeit* and to learning. What are they going to do with that?"

Yaakov sighed. "Okay," he said.

The psychologist looked up as Ari came into the room. "I have analyzed your tests, Ari, and I want to discuss them with you before we talk to your father."

Ari smiled gratefully. Though he knew that he had done well on the intelligence test, he had enough insight to realize that the personality tests revealed much of his inner world. He wondered what the psychologist would say.

"Ari, firstly, I want to say that as far as a university education stands, which is what your father wishes for you, you are capable of doing well in just about any course you choose. Your I.Q. level is very superior, very, very superior, and it is consistent on all the different aspects of intelligence which I tested. You are very creative, highly perceptive. Your social intelligence is very superior. In fact, you would probably make a very good psychologist," she smiled.

"But that isn't you, is it, Ari? Forcing you to study in those directions would be a waste of time, wouldn't it? You are in love with Torah study, I can see that. And though I am not at all *frum* myself, it is obvious in all the tests that this is what motivates and inspires you. You aren't going to be satisfied with secular learning, are you?"

It was Ari's turn to smile. Not a bad psychological assessment, he thought to himself.

"Your father also asked me to assess if your attachment to religion is unhealthy, and if it could possibly be the loss of your mother which drove you to it."

Ari held his breath. What was she about to say?

"Your mother's death did affect you very deeply. It was extremely traumatic, as was the divorce so many years earlier. There are many problems in your relationship with your father and stepmother. But at the same time, you seem to belong, as it were, to another family, a very healthy family in itself, where you have found warmth, stability, peace and acceptance."

"The Levys," said Ari. "The rabbi's family."

Ari liked what he was hearing. Yes, it was true. As much as he belonged to his own family, he felt he belonged with the Levys. He accepted them and was accepted as part of the family. Even after Yaakov had left for *yeshivah*, Ari was there on a daily basis, learning with the rabbi. Though he cooked a little for himself at home, he also ate with the Levys fairly regularly, and spent most *Shabbosos* with them. Yes, this was his second home, maybe in many ways, his first.

"Your attachment to religion isn't abnormal or unhealthy. It definitely is the center of your life, but not in a sick or distorted way. I would say that you are psychologically very healthy and normal."

Ari smiled and gave an exaggerated sigh of relief.

"In fact, many of your personality qualities are on a superior level. In other words," she said, "you're okay. You are more than okay, and my recommendation would be that you go to *yeshivah*. Do you want to discuss anything, or shall we call your father in?"

The metric results were out. Ari had obtained several distinctions, and was immediately offered scholarships to various universities. His parents had seen his results with pride, and again his father had tried to make him see reason.

"I am proud of you son, very, very proud of you, and all my colleagues and friends are proud of you. But you are wasting your potential and throwing it down the drain. I know what that psychologist said, and I don't know how you persuaded her to recommend that you go to *yeshivah*, quite against my wish. And then she goes and charges me several hundred rand for giving the advice I didn't want her to give.

"In spite of that, I think you should go to university. You have golden opportunities in your hands which you are throwing away. It is a sin. The Creator has given you a brain and talents, and you throw them into His face and say you don't want to use them."

"I really want to go to *yeshivah gedolah,* Dad," said Ari. "And if you force me to go to university, I will stop as soon as I am twenty-one and I will go to *yeshivah*. It will only be wasting time going to university."

"But son," said his father, "I let you go to Yeshivah High School. I thought that would get this out of your system. You have had enough of these religious studies. I mean, you had them all the way through high school. No one knows as much as you do, not among my friends, anyway. You know enough. Branch out into something new and interesting. Let your mind go free, and not be tangled up with this ancient nonsense. What do these rabbis know about the modern world? I mean, those laws were outdated years and years ago. Who keeps them except you and a few other rabbis?

"Anthony, son, why don't you give it a chance, just for a year? Take a break from this religion thing and just be normal, just for a year.

"Go to clubs and parties like all the other boys your age. Eat out where you like. Please, for my sake, see what life is like when one acts normally."

Ari looked at his watch. It was nearly *Minchah* time.

"Sorry, Dad, we'll discuss it later," said Ari, and within minutes he was gone.

David Isaacson sank into one of the armchairs. Why did his son have to be so obstinate? Couldn't he give just a little? Why was he so selfish when it came to his religion? Couldn't he cooperate with the family on anything? Couldn't he join them in any of their social affairs without making them thoroughly embarrassed by not eating or walking out if there was dancing or if a woman was singing? Why couldn't he be normal?

The boy had an excellent mind. He could excel in any field he wanted. The psychologist had made it clear. Oh, why was the boy so stubborn?

He would make sure that his other two children made full use of their talents, and as he thought about that another anxiety flooded his mind.

Debby was not too influenced by her brother. She had begun ballet lessons some years back, and had done very well. Her life was tied up with concerts and practice and lessons. But he was worried about Jules. Only a week ago, his wife had repeated to him a very disturbing statement made by Jules.

"When I am *bar-mitzvah*, I am going to be religious like Ari."

It was true that he still had almost two years until his *bar-mitzvah*, but Sheila had been very upset, and she had begged her husband to do something about it. She did not want her son to be under Ari's influence.

At that moment, she came into the room, her face flushed.

"David," she said, "your son is finished metric now, and I have tolerated him enough in the house."

He turned to her sharply, anger flaming up inside him.

"I thought you got on quite well with him," he said. "Have you been pretending all this time?"

"No," she said. "I haven't. I do like him. But I can't have him influencing Jules."

"He's still a kid," said Mr. Isaacson. "He sees his big brother as a hero."

"Anthony was still a kid when he came here," she said. "He

never got over the influence of the rabbi."

"But we'll send him to a different rabbi," said her husband. "He doesn't have to go near the Levys."

"He is already quite friendly with Zevi Levy," snapped his wife. "He has his *bar-mitzvah* lessons all planned out. He wants to start quite soon."

"We'll delay it," said Mr. Isaacson. "Don't worry about it."

"I have to worry about it," said Sheila, almost on the verge of tears. "Jules told me that he has decided to stop eating meat in this house. He told me my kitchen was *treif.*"

"Jules said that?" said his father.

"Yes," she said. "I want your son out. He has finished his schooling now."

"Then he must accept the scholarship to Rhodes," said his father. "Grahamstown is several hundred kilometers away."

"Rhodes almost has more holidays than term time," said Sheila. "My brother went there. I think he was home around four months a year, all in all. I want him away, maybe even at that *yeshivah* he wants to go to. Yaakov came home for *Pesach,* a few days over *Rosh Hashanah* and three weeks now in December. And Anthony never stays with us during *Pesach* anyway, because he won't even drink a glass of water here.

"Please, David, for the sake of *our* children, send him away to Johannesburg!"

Thirteen

Within several months time, Ari once again became Yaakov's *chavrusa*. Although Ari had entered the *yeshivah gedolah* a full year after Yaakov, his clarity of mind and his ability to grasp all sides of a *Gemara pilpul*, and relate them to other tractates where similar subjects were being discussed, made him a student who could not go unnoticed. He quickly became a match for anyone in the *yeshivah*.

People who did not know his background assumed that he came from a long line of rabbis. When they did find out, they were stunned.

"Look at Rabbi Yochanan and Resh Lakish," said Ari, if anyone commented on his and Yaakov's differing backgrounds.

Early in Yeshivah High School, Ari had become fascinated by Resh Lakish, the bandit leader who had become drawn to Torah by the light emanating from Rabbi Yochanan's face. He had become his student and then his *chavrusa*. That and the story of Rabbi Akiva, who hadn't begun his Torah studies until the age of forty, had given him a great deal of encouragement.

He thought back on his first few days in the *yeshivah gedolah.* Even though Yaakov had been there, he had felt incredibly lonely and homesick when he arrived. He had neither his home nor the Levy home to go to, and it felt strange being in a dorm with other young men. He was suddenly on his own with his own responsibilities.

He had often longed for the days when he would be free from the constant anti-*Yiddishkeit* input he was experiencing from his family, but he found in his first few days that he even missed that.

Ari's uncertainty and homesickness began to fade as he became enthralled with the experience of being able to learn for a full day and explore the richness and depth of the *Gemara.*

As he went on, he realized that what he had done at Yeshivah High School had only been an introduction, paddling, as it were, in the sea of Torah. Now he became engrossed in and thirsty for its waters as he waded deeper and deeper into them.

Rabbi Weinstein, the *Rosh Yeshivah,* watched Ari carefully. He had heard reports from the high school about his brilliance in both *Limudei Kodesh* and secular studies, and he had heard the boy's rabbi, Yaakov's father, talk about Ari's self-sacrifice for his Torah studies. He was to expect an outstanding *bachur*, and he had not been disappointed. He had instinctively liked this somewhat shy but, at the same time, forceful young man with the striking green eyes and the jet black hair.

Though Ari had not, on their first interview, pushed himself in any way, the Rabbi had been aware already of the sharpness of Ari's mind, the sincerity of his commitment.

Over the months he had been struck by his qualities of character. Had living in a situation so contrary to *Yiddishkeit* for so long strengthened what was good in him?

Though at that time Ari was one of the youngest in the *yeshivah* and in the dorm, he also showed clear leadership qualities. When asked to help on *Shabbos* with the youth *minyan* at one of the *shuls*, he was a powerful inspiration and influence to the boys, many of whom started to take their *Yiddishkeit* seriously after he had been working with them.

Strangely enough, since he had left home, Ari found himself thinking a great deal about his mother. He kept the framed picture of her with him as a child on his bureau. He wondered what life would have been like if she hadn't died. He might be working in her curio shop on the South Coast of Natal, having hardly any awareness of *Yiddishkeit*. What kind of *bar-mitzvah* would he have had? Would he have found a friend in the rabbi, as he had with Rabbi Levy? And what would his mother have said about it?

For some reason, he also found himself dreaming about her. Sometimes she would be talking to him as they made coffee together in the kitchen as they had always done. At other times, they would be in the ambulance, flying along the South Coast Road.

Ari was becoming close to the Weinstein family, and became a regular visitor in their home. All the *yeshivah bachurim* had a certain amount of contact with the *Rosh Yeshivah's* family, but for some reason, Ari was invited for *Shabbos* more often than others. Was it that they felt he needed more contact with a family?

He felt grateful to them in that they had perceived that he needed to be close to them. Perhaps they felt sorry for him because he had lost his mother, and his father and step-mother were not *frum*. It did not for a moment ever cross his mind that the *Rosh Yeshivah* saw him as someone outstanding, both in terms of his learning ability and his *midos*, and for that he had taken a special interest in him.

Meanwhile, Ari was getting letters from home on a regular basis, especially from Jules and Debby. Debby's letters were full of ballet news. She had been chosen for the star part in a concert, and she could not contain her excitement and her delight and pride. It was to be held in several weeks' time. There were to be three performances: one on Friday night, one on Saturday afternoon and one on Saturday night.

At first, Ari felt at a loss about how to respond. Eventually, he congratulated her for being chosen, but wrote that he had felt upset that two of the concerts had been on *Shabbos*.

To this letter he had received a rather aggressive reply from Aunt Sheila, saying that this was Debby's big chance, and how could he upset her so much about it?

Jules' letters were about school, about cricket and a little about his struggle with becoming more observant of Judaism. At one point, Jules wrote that he had stopped playing cricket because the team played on Saturday. Ari waited for the torrent of written words which would surely pour onto his head. But it didn't come, and in Jules' next letter he said that he had just told Mummy and Daddy that he had stopped playing cricket and wanted to take photography instead.

He also asked Ari please to send him stamps, as he was about to start a stamp collection and he needed to swap stamps with Zevi.

Ari wondered how much contact Jules actually had with Zevi. He couldn't imagine it could be much.

It also took him by surprise when he learned, by a comment in Jules' letter, that the child had, in fact, stopped eating meat. He wondered what the reaction had been about it. After the fury about his letter to Debby about dancing on *Shabbos*, he didn't write too openly to Jules, otherwise their contact might somehow be cut off. He did manage, however, to send him a few pamphlets with stories and fun pages for Jewish children. Jules never acknowledged them, and Ari wondered if he had ever received them.

Ari did not go home for *Pesach* that year, even though Yaakov did. Several *bachurim*, especially those from overseas, stayed in the dorm over *Pesach* and ate with various members of the community. Ari spent both *sedarim* with the Weinsteins.

He kept up a very active correspondence with the Levys. In fact, they quite often commented that they heard from him more often than from Yaakov. Ari was well aware that Yaakov had never been one for writing letters. Yaakov had, however, returned home for both *Pesach* and *Rosh Hashanah*. Ari planned to go only for the longer December holidays.

As the time drew near, however, he found himself becoming more and more apprehensive, alternating between that and a good feeling at the thought of once again being able to spend time with the Levys.

FOURTEEN

"Anthony, you've grown! I would hardly have recognized you! You look years older. I mean, with that beginning of a beard! What made you grow it?"

Ari's father, who met him at the airport, looked a little embarrassed as he welcomed his *yeshivah bachur* son. He had not expected him to look quite so rabbinic. Mr. Isaacson felt embarrassed as he helped his son take his luggage to the car.

"Thanks for your letters, son. We really missed you. It is good that you are going to spend a few weeks with us. You really look much, much older. I mean, with that beard, you make me feel quite ancient!"

Everything in his tone said, "I hope you are going to shave off that beard while you are here," but Ari ignored this.

"It's so good to be with you again, Dad," he said. "I'm so glad to be in a place with the sea and the mountains, instead of being surrounded by mine dumps and buildings."

"Yes, I always miss the surroundings when I leave Cape Town," said his father. "But you are happy where you are, aren't you? I mean, you are going back next year?"

"Of course, Dad. I'm going to be there several years, please G-d."

His father seemed to give a sigh of relief. As they drove home, he seemed a little preoccupied, as though there was something he had to say before they arrived.

"Anthony, I don't know how to put this, but Sheila and I have talked it over and I must tell you." He paused, embarrassed. "Anthony, it isn't that we don't love you. Of course we do, but Anthony, I have to look after my wife and the rest of the family. You are already grown up, as it were."

"I understand that, Dad," said Ari, wondering what his father was trying to say.

"You have taken a very strange path in life, my son, and we have kind of accepted the fact that you want to be different, and to separate yourself from people. But we have other children," he went on, "and we want them to grow up normal, to be like everyone around them. We don't want them dressing as if they come from the last century, or acting as if G-d is around every minute of the day, worrying about every detail of their actions. You have such an odd concept of G-d, Anthony. He isn't concerned about what you eat or the way you dress or whether you phone a friend on Saturday. G-d is concerned with bigger things, like the way you treat people and your philosophy of life."

"Hashem *is* everywhere," said Ari. "And He is concerned with everything we do and everything we think."

"Do you think that He has time for all that?" said his father. "Anyway, Anthony, we don't have that kind of G-d, thank goodness. Ours is a G-d of love who doesn't mind what you do, as long as you don't hurt anyone else, as long as you are happy. He most definitely doesn't mind what you eat. We don't want you to come preaching at the children and upsetting them. Your letter to Debby shocked us completely. The child was delighted with her achievement, and here you come and pour cold water on the whole thing by trying to give her a guilt complex. *Our* G-d was very happy she worked so hard and was chosen for the ballet."

He went on, his face beginning to flush and his hand to tremble.

"And Jules," he said. "I am far more worried about Jules. I don't want to lose him like we've lost you. Anthony, I want you to speak to him. He thinks you are the greatest because you are his big brother. I want you to tell him that he doesn't need to do all these things, that he must eat what his mother makes for him. After all, isn't one of the Ten Commandments 'Honor your father and your mother'? You see, I also know what the Torah says. All we want is a normal son."

Ari was quiet. He obviously could not agree to do this, nor could he at this point mention that one could not negate the *mitzvos* of the Torah in order to honor one's parents. He actually could not think of what to say.

His father's attitude suddenly softened. "Don't worry son, it is good to have you home. Just remember what I have said."

Aunt Sheila greeted him warmly, and in fact said she rather liked his beginnings of a beard, commenting on how he had matured.

Debby and Jules were beside themselves with excitement, saying they had counted the days until he came home. Debby immediately produced her ballet costumes for him to see, saying that they had bought a ticket for him for the Saturday night concert because she knew he couldn't come on Friday night. Ari thought he would settle in a little before he told her that a girl's ballet performance wasn't the appropriate place for a *yeshivah bachur.*

Jules immediately announced that from now on, he wanted to be called Yehudah, a comment which acted like a quick-freeze mechanism on the room.

"You see, Anthony?" said his father. "You have to be the one to stop this. I would never have given him a name like that at his circumcision if I had thought he would ever actually use it."

"We can't have another son growing up in this odd way," said Aunt Sheila, all her cordiality vanishing. "You look as though you have grown up a bit. Perhaps you can undo the harm you have done to this boy."

Jules seemed, for some reason, to be oblivious to his parents' distress, though Ari was soon to learn that it did in fact upset him very deeply.

He spoke to Ari later on that evening, knocking quietly on his door so that others in the house would not know he was with him.

"Ari," he said, "I want to be *frum*, really, really *frum*. Mummy and Daddy are very much against it. They say such terrible things about you and about the rabbi and about Yaakov, and now even about Zevi. I went to see Zevi the other day, and I have been grounded since then. I am hardly allowed to go out of the house at all and it's holidays now, which is awful.

"And Ari, one day I am going to be *bar-mitzvah*, and I want to do the right thing. My parents want me to go to Reform. That won't be good, will it? Even they have never been to Reform, but they say that even the rabbi doesn't bother about what he eats, so he certainly won't interfere with anything I eat."

Ari gave a sigh. It was good to see that Jules, or Yehudah as he wanted to be called, was becoming more and more involved with *Yiddishkeit*, but he foresaw a very hard time ahead for him. He himself had never really forgotten the hurtful things that had been said to him. He remembered what Rabbi Levy had advised.

"Yehudah," he said, noting his brother's face light up as he used his Hebrew name. "Dad and Mum will say all kinds of terrible things to you, as they did to me, and it will hurt you a lot."

A look of pain crossed the boy's face. "They have hurt me already," he said quietly.

"You must remember, Yehudah, that what they say isn't really directed at you. It is directed at their own relationship with Judaism. They are bothered so much because a Jew has a Jewish soul which can be satisfied only with Torah. They keep having to say to that Jewish soul, 'Keep quiet! I don't want to hear you. I am busy with my life.'

"And you, Yehudah, keep reminding them about their Jewish soul, so they say to you 'Keep quiet, I don't want to hear you.'" He wondered if Yehudah could grasp what he was saying.

"Thanks, Ari," said the boy. "You mean they are shouting at the Torah to leave them alone, because Hashem keeps calling them to keep it, and they are not really shouting at me."

"Yes, Yehudah, you've got it," said Ari. "But that is when you are being shouted at for doing something Jewish, not when you are doing something naughty!"

Yehudah suddenly gave a mischievous grin. "That figures," he said. "You mean when they were shouting at me because I cut off half my sister's braid, they weren't shouting at the Torah."

"No," said Ari, "they were shouting at you." He smiled. "What did Debby say, and what on earth made you do that?"

"Well, Debby half made me do it. She gave me a pair of

scissors and asked me to trim her hair at the end of the braid. So I did it, and it wasn't straight. So I did it again, and it wasn't straight on the other side, so I . . ."

"Cut off half the braid," finished Ari.

"Yes," said Yehudah. "Everyone was cross with me, very, very cross with me, and Debby was crying and shouting and asking Dad to shave off my hair and eyebrows, and she would have done it herself if she hadn't had to go to the hairdresser very urgently."

The two brothers rocked with laughter, forgetting that their being together would hardly be approved of by their father, and indeed Mr. Isaacson did appear in the room looking somewhat flustered.

"What are you two boys laughing about?" he demanded.

"He was telling me the story of Debby's braid, or Debby's half braid," Ari said, still laughing.

His father backed away. That didn't sound too religious. In fact it sounded somewhat irreligious to him. Perhaps Anthony wouldn't be so bad with him after all. He started somewhat uncertainly to leave the room, and then seemed to want to share something with his sons.

"I didn't quite do that when I was a boy," he said. "But in a science lesson once, there was a girl sitting in front of me who had long, dark brown braids that used to brush into my desk. I found that very irritating, so one day I put the end of one of them into a bottle of ammonia and peroxide I had brought, and it became blonde. Everybody behind me laughed and laughed because they saw me doing it. The girl was so mad. So was the teacher, and so was the principal. At least I think he was. But I do remember that when the teacher and the girl marched me out, almost by one ear, and showed the principal the braid, he put his hand over his mouth because he was so angry. But now, when I think back over it, I think he had to stop himself from laughing."

Both boys laughed, and father and sons sat for almost an hour swapping school stories.

At one stage, Sheila came in, but left. Ari had changed. Before he had left for Johannesburg, he had not been able to really laugh like that, at least, not in her house, she thought a little guiltily.

FIFTEEN

Almost two years passed before Ari went home again. He had grown into a handsome young man whose eyes reflected his complete involvement in Torah study.

His last holiday, although he enjoyed good times spent with Rabbi Levy, had been very trying. His family had subjected him and his brother Yehudah to jibes and mockery.

Even during those times when the family had been pleasant, even accepting, there had been an undercurrent of antagonism and resentment.

He discussed this at length with Rabbi Levy and with his *rosh yeshivah*, and both agreed that Ari should keep a good but distant relationship with his parents, and to visit as infrequently as possible. Although Yehudah needed him in many ways, he could keep up a good, regular correspondence with him.

On the occasions that Yaakov went down to Cape Town, he would make it a point to speak to Yehudah and to encourage him. At one stage, Yaakov discovered that Yehudah was actually managing somehow to learn regularly with Zevi. He was quite sure the Isaacsons did not know about it, and he wondered how Yehudah had managed to organize it.

Ari received a very aggressive, scathing letter from his stepmother, saying that his influence was being felt even from a distance, and that she wished he had never set foot in her home, that if she had known she had given a home to a viper, she would have refused and he would have gone to an orphanage.

He was very upset and angry about the letter, and thought about it constantly.

Eventually, he wrote to Rabbi Levy, ashamed to talk to someone about it face to face in the *yeshivah*. He couldn't tell them that in the middle of learning, thoughts would spring into his head about wicked stepmothers, causing him to become so angry that he couldn't concentrate.

Rabbi Levy didn't respond directly about his stepmother, but quoted to him an English expression, "You can't stop birds flying over your head, but you can stop them making a nest in your hair."

"In other words, all kinds of thoughts come into a person's mind, which cannot be prevented," continued the rabbi. "What is not good however, is when a person dwells on these thoughts, inviting them in, so to speak, and spends hours thinking about them. A person can control these thoughts before they take hold of him."

Ari quickly took his *rav's* advice to heart, and when the thoughts troubled him again, he deliberately switched his mind onto what he was learning. He found that in fact, he could stop thinking about it. His anger eventually abated until it disappeared.

He discussed it with Yaakov, showing him his father's answer.

"I can understand why you get angry," he said. "I used to wonder why you didn't years ago. I was quite impressed with the way you handled it, because they were often so rude to you."

Ari found that once again he could think about his stepmother without all kinds of resentment. It hadn't been worth it. The anger had taken a toll on himself and his learning more than anything else.

He would not allow it to happen again.

About six months before Yehudah's *bar-mitzvah*, after Yehudah had flatly refused to go to Reform, Mr. Isaacson got in touch with the Great Synagogue and enrolled him in the *bar-mitzvah* classes. The rabbi had been a little upset at the late registration, but his upset turned to surprise as he realized that the new student was, in fact, quite knowledgeable, in many respects far ahead of many of the other class members. He eventually found out the full story from his colleague, Rabbi Levy, and the *melamdim* took a special interest in the boy, responding to his enthusiasm and his obvious sincerity.

It was now time for the *bar-mitzvah*, and Ari was to fly down to Cape Town for five days to be with the family for the occasion.

He had been advised to make it a short trip, the main reason being that the *yeshivah* was not on vacation at that time.

Once again, his father met him at the airport, and was overawed at the change in his son.

Somewhere deep inside, he was rather proud of Ari, but he quickly put that out of his mind. He would have preferred another engineer!

They chatted amicably on the way home. Jules' *bar-mitzvah* was at the Great Synagogue. There was to be an evening reception in a nearby hotel. The rabbi had suggested to the family that they all stay in the hotel from Friday afternoon until Sunday morning, and the Isaacsons had rather liked the idea.

Ari gave a sigh of relief. He realized immediately that Yehudah's *bar-mitzvah* was on a far more elegant scale than his own, but he felt no resentment, only relief that it was to be a kosher *bar-mitzvah*.

Sheila greeted Ari cordially, obviously preferring not to refer to her letter which had upset him so much. He, in turn, did not mention it nor show the slightest hint of bitterness about it. That was best for all concerned, he had no doubt.

To his surprise and delight, his brother cooked him a simple meal on his own hotplate. Ari noticed that his brother had bought only foods with reliable *kashrus* supervision.

"How long have you been preparing your own food, Yehudah?" he asked in amazement.

"Well," said his younger brother, somewhat philosophically, "several months ago, Mum got sort of worried about me because I would hardly eat her cooking. I went with her to the supermarket and saw all kinds of things I had seen in the Levy's house. We bought them and I began to cook them myself, using your hotplate. You had labelled all the utensils, so I knew which ones were milk and which were *parve*.

"It was very difficult, though. You could go to the Levys. I hardly ever get there. If I mention Zevi Levy, Mum starts crying."

"Crying?" said Ari, somewhat horrified.

"Yes," said Yehudah. "The worst thing is to wake up in the middle of the night and hear her crying and telling Dad that she's lost me to religion. I mean, I'm not going anywhere, except of course to *yeshivah*. But I will always be back. I know I'm doing the right thing, but I feel guilty for hurting Mum."

"That's awful," said Ari, sympathetically. "No wonder she is cross with me."

"Yes, you are the big, bad influence," said Yehudah, laughing. "But you haven't been here for a long time, so I don't see how she can blame you."

"What have you been doing about learning, and things like that?"

Yehudah took him to his room and shut the door and locked it.

"Look," he said. He went over to his bookcase, to his set of encyclopedias and took out four of them. Behind them, a space of about three inches ran all the way behind the encyclopedias, to the back of the bookcase. This was filled with Jewish books. Without removing the encyclopedias it was impossible to find them, and who else in the house would want to look at encyclopedias?

"*Chumash, Tehillim, Siddur, Mishnayos, Ein Yaakov*—where did you get all these?" asked Ari in wonderment. In front of the books he saw the names 'Yaakov Levy' or 'Zevi Levy'.

Debby insisted he look at her ballet cups. She was friendly and happy to see him and not a little proud of him. However, she seemed oblivious to anything Jewish, except as a passing interest. She knew about Yehudah's book collection and of his visits to the Levys and kept it strictly a secret. Ari admired her for that.

The *bar-mitzvah* was a great success. Yehudah read quite a lot of his *parshah* and the *haftorah*. Rabbi Rosenberg was obviously very impressed with him, his star student, and he did not hesitate to mention this in his speech. He also stressed that Yehudah was a young man who had devoted himself to the practice as well as the philosophy of Judaism, a statement which made the Isaacsons somewhat uneasy.

The celebration at the hotel was lavish, with a band and

hundreds of guests. Yehudah, the man of the moment, gave a speech that had impressed many. Though he did not make the public commitment to a Torah life style, as Ari had done, he left no doubt in the minds of his listeners that he was committed in this direction.

As he sat down amidst much applause, he announced that his brother Ari would now speak.

Though he had not been officially asked to speak, Ari was not surprised, and he had prepared a few points on the *parshah*, which he presented in a clear, gentle commanding way. His sincerity combined with his speaking talents, and use of language, would have captured any audience, regardless of the subject.

Mr. Isaacson could not help but feel an overwhelming flood of pride in his older son.

SIXTEEN

Ari was nearing the end of his *davening*. He was feeling unhappy with himself because once again, he found his mind wandering during *Shemoneh Esrei*. He tried hard to concentrate, but halfway through, his mind just wandered off. He had to draw himself back from Table Mountain in order to catch the last few words.

Did that happen to everyone? Surely not. In fact, did that happen to anyone else in the *yeshivah*? He looked around him. Everyone seemed to be totally intent on what they were doing. Why did this happen to him? Was it because he was not *frum* from birth?

Why was it that sometimes, no matter how hard he tried, he would find his mind wandering on to all kinds of things?

Guiltily he continued and finished his *davening*. Perhaps one day he should speak to someone about it, or perhaps he should write to Rabbi Levy. He felt too embarrassed to admit this to anyone in the *yeshivah*. Perhaps it did happen to everyone, or at least to some people. Perhaps that was why *davening* was called service of the heart, because you had to work at it.

But there was his mind wandering again, even if it was wandering about wandering!

Just as he was finishing breakfast, Yerachmiel, one of the *bachurim*, gave him the message that Rabbi Weinstein wanted to see him in his office. Ari's heart began to beat faster. Was something wrong? It was unusual for a *bachur* to be summoned in this way. The *rosh yeshivah* was in contact with the *bachurim* constantly, but hardly ever on formal interview level. Had something, Heaven forbid, happened to his father?

He *bentched* quickly and was soon standing outside the office door. He hadn't felt like this since he was first in *yeshivah*. Had he done something wrong? Was there something wrong?

But the rabbi's warm smile as he entered the room reassured him. No, this was not to be an unpleasant interview. But what?

Rabbi Weinstein motioned Ari to sit down, and seemed to be assessing him for a few seconds.

"Ari," he began, "have you given any thought to the question of a *shidduch*?"

Ari blushed crimson. He didn't answer the question and the rabbi, in fact, did not seem to expect an answer.

"I have been thinking about a *shidduch* for you," said the rabbi. "Actually, I have someone in mind."

Ari wished his hands would stop shaking, that his heart would stop beating so fast and that his face would return to a normal color. He looked at the rabbi, but could not trust himself to speak. What was a *bachur* supposed to say, anyway? He suddenly felt very vulnerable and immature.

The rabbi continued to speak. He had seen just this

reaction in scores of *bachurim*. Even the bravest *bachur* trembled at the thought of going out on the first *shidduch*.

"I have a good friend who is a *rosh yeshivah* in England. He has a daughter."

Ari frowned. A *rosh yeshivah's* daughter! She would most definitely be a girl from a long line of rabbis and rebbetzins. He had no *yichus* to speak of. How could Rabbi Weinstein be suggesting this?

The rabbi immediately saw Ari's puzzlement and hesitation. In fact, he had expected it.

He tactfully put it into words.

"Ari, are you worried because you and the young woman, Brocha, come from different backgrounds?" The rabbi continued. "Yes, Brocha comes from a rabbinic background, and you don't. Rabbi Goldstein, her father, is a very special man, besides being a *talmid chacham* of note. He sees *yichus* as very important. However, he sees other factors as equally important, factors which you, Ari, have in abundance. In fact, the rabbi's eldest son-in-law was a brilliant student from a background somewhat similar to yours. He is now the rabbi's right-hand man.

"You have been *frum*, Ari, ever since you became *bar-mitzvah*, ever since you were completely answerable, as it were, for your actions."

He paused. Ari was still looking very nervous and flushed, but he seemed to have settled down a little.

"Rabbi and Mrs. Goldstein and their daughters will be in Johannesburg in just over three weeks' time," he said. "The rabbi will be on business here for his *yeshivah*. Can I arrange for you to meet?"

Ari's voice, when it came out, was almost hoarse from his nervousness.

"Yes . . . uh, yes," he said at last, relieved that he had three weeks to get used to the idea. At least it wasn't three days or three hours. He would have time to speak to Rabbi Levy and Yaakov and find out what he had to do and say.

Suddenly he smiled. "Thank you," he said. "It really means a lot that you would do this for me. I hope I won't disappoint you."

"I am sure you won't," said Rabbi Weinstein.

He walked out of the office wondering what anyone would say if they saw him. He was sure he was still blushing and he kept smiling to himself. Fortunately, the first person he ran into was Yaakov.

"Ari, what's happened?" asked Yaakov. "You look as though you've just been chosen to represent South African Jewry in America, and you are sort of scared, but thrilled."

"That's right," said Ari.

"You've been chosen to go to America to represent . . ." Yaakov repeated, incredulously.

"No, of course not," said Ari. "I am kind of scared, but thrilled."

Yaakov looked at him carefully and Ari blushed.

"A *shidduch*?" he whispered.

"Yes," said Ari. "Yaakov, have you been out on a *shidduch*?"

"No," said Yaakov. "My father wants me to learn overseas first, and then meet someone over there. Sometimes I think he has someone in mind, but he never answers any of my questions about it. But what about you?" he asked, a delighted tone creeping into his voice. "Did Rabbi Weinstein arrange something? When are you going out?"

Ari told him everything the rabbi had told him, and Yaakov gave a low whistle.

"That means he thinks you are an outstanding *bachur*," said Yaakov, quite matter-of-factly. "I mean, that's quite a *shidduch* he is making for you."

"But what do I say to her?" asked Ari. "I mean, what do girls talk about? You know, you've got sisters."

"Oh, they fight," said Yaakov. "I'm sure it's sort of different in a *shidduch*. I mean, you have to be very, very polite and find out all about one another, apart from what you've been told and everything. The first subject you can discuss is the Jewish community in South Africa and the Jewish community in England. That should take at least an hour."

"An hour!" said Ari. "I don't have to talk to her for an hour, do I? That's a long time to talk to a girl."

"At least two hours," said Yaakov ominously.

"It will be two hours of silence," said Ari, dolefully.

"Ari," said Yaakov, "I've never been on a *shidduch*. I'm not really the person to advise you. Maybe you ought to phone my father."

Ari breathed a sigh of relief. "That's a great idea," he said. "Do you think he'll be surprised that I'll be meeting someone?"

"I'm quite sure he knows," said Yaakov. "Rabbi Weinstein would never have organized a *shidduch* for you without contacting him. I am sure he was the first to know."

SEVENTEEN

“Tatty, I am interested. Very, very interested.” Brocha’s dark eyes sparkled and her face was still a little flushed from the effect of her first meeting with Ari. “He’s special, Tatty, he’s really special.”

“I know that, Brochie,” said her father, thrilled by her reaction. He had spoken to Ari at length, and had been more than satisfied with the *shidduch*. He found him to be a truly outstanding *bachur*, both in learning and in *midos*.

“I want you to meet him a few more times before you decide,” he said. “I want you to be absolutely sure. After all, this is the first *shidduch* you have been out on.”

Her mother came into the room, and Brocha went over to her and kissed her.

“How did it go, my girl?” she asked.

“He was fabulous!” she said. “He’s the kind of person I would really like to spend my life with!”

“Give it time,” said her mother, extremely pleased at her daughter’s positive reaction. She had also been very impressed with Ari, and felt she would like him as a son-in-law, but she didn't want Brocha to rush.

"Brochie, you were very nervous when you went in. What did you talk to him about?"

"Let me tell you all about it," she said, relieved to be able to confide in her parents.

"Both of us were very shy at first. It was his first *shidduch* too. At first we talked about what we were each learning, and after that, we weren't so shy, and we talked about all kinds of other things. I told him about seminary and the girls there, and he told me about Cape Town and Durban and about how his mother died."

"He told you about that?" asked her father in surprise.

"Well, he wasn't going to, I don't think," she said, "but it came out. It must have been a terrible, terrible shock to him. But he changed the subject when he saw that I was getting upset."

"And you really liked him?" her mother said.

"Yes, yes of course I did," she said. "We will meet again tomorrow and speak some more."

At the same time as Brocha was speaking to her parents, Rabbi and Mrs. Weinstein were very seriously speaking to Ari. He had come over the house announcing to them that Brocha was the girl he wanted to marry, but he supposed they should meet another few times just to be sure.

"I know it's the right thing, though," he kept repeating.

Rabbi Weinstein reminded him that this was his first *shidduch,* and that he had to think very carefully.

The engagement was three weeks later, several days before *Chanukah.*

Ari felt that he had never been so happy in his whole life. Every time he looked at Brocha he wanted to rub his eyes to make sure he was not dreaming. How could such an exceptional girl from such an outstanding family agree to marry him? How could it be that he was becoming the son-in-law of the *rosh yeshivah* of one of the largest *yeshivos* in England? How could it be that he would have a mother-in-law like Rebbetzin Goldstein, a scholar in her own right, and one of the warmest, most motherly people he had ever met?

Ari phoned his parents and told them about Brocha. They were thrilled, but turned down his invitation to fly up for the engagement party, as Mr. Isaacson could not free himself from his business commitments.

They invited Ari to come down to them with Brocha, but he preferred to wait until after she returned to England. He would visit on the second day of *Chanukah*, and would stay with them over *Shabbos Chanukah* and for a few days afterwards.

Ari asked his father to mark his calendar for the forthcoming year for early in *Nissan*, before *Pesach*. He wanted his parents to come to England for the wedding and for *sheva brachos*, but Mr. Isaacson gave a very non-committal answer.

Yaakov was overjoyed about the *shidduch*. He saw his friend change into a confident, happy person with a quick sense of humor. He seemed to have attained, even in all the excitement, a certain tranquillity.

The engagement party was well-attended and celebrated with great *simchah*. Everyone was happy for Ari. All who knew him had been impressed with him and they agreed that the daughter of Rabbi Goldstein seemed to be a most suitable partner for him.

Ari felt that he had never experienced a happier day in his life. It seemed that life was surpassing his most unattainable dreams.

EIGHTEEN

"Fasten your seat belts. We are about to land in Cape Town. The time is one o'clock a.m., temperature seventeen degrees. We hope you had a pleasant trip."

Ari and Yaakov always enjoyed the midnight flight. Besides the fact that it was nearly half price, there was something about landing in a city in which nearly everyone was asleep that was quite exciting. The lights twinkled beneath them, except for the large patch of darkness which was Table Mountain, and the darkness which at that moment was to their left, which was the sea.

Ari had a longing to go on the cableway up the mountainside once again. He would love to show Brocha this magnificent sight. He knew she would be thrilled to see the massive, flat-topped mountain sculptured from sandstone, rising more than a thousand meters above the bay.

He had heard that from end to end, the flat top summit measured nearly three kilometers. On less clear days, the heights were hidden from view, and the clouds covering it formed a kind of tablecloth. Hundreds of different species of plants and flowers could be found on the slopes of the mountain, and at times one could meet all kinds of animals, such as baboons, lynx and porcupines.

He knew Brocha would love Cape Town. He would take her to the beachfront suburbs differing so much in character from one another, as if the Atlantic and Indian Oceans gave them a character of their own. And he would take her to Cape Agulhas, Africa's most southerly point, where the two oceans meet.

The bump of the plane onto the ground jolted Ari back to reality.

Shortly after the plane landed, they hoisted their overnight bags from the roof racks, said good-bye to the people around them and followed the crowd along the aisle to the exit.

Ari kept thinking to himself that sometime before *Pesach*, just before his wedding, he and his parents would be getting off a plane in England. Rabbi Weinstein would be with them, too. He had promised to come to the wedding.

The thought of that occasion made him smile all the way to the door, and to totally ignore the fact that he nearly tripped over a bag protruding into the aisle.

"Careful," said Yaakov. "I know you are dreaming of Heathrow Airport and of a certain wedding to be held in England early *Nissan*, but don't break your neck before you get there. Come back to earth!"

They were now out of the plane and were walking towards the arrivals hall.

"Yaakov," said Ari, "I've never had a kosher home before, a really Jewish home. I have never been part of a *frum* family before. I know I was part of your family in many ways, but this is different. I can't believe this is really happening to me. I just can't believe it! I have just never been so happy before."

They were met, to both Ari's and Yaakov's surprise, by Rabbi Levy and Mr. Isaacson, who had arrived in the same car and were looking quite cordial in their relationship. Had things changed so much? They wanted to see photographs of Ari's engagement, and he was more than happy to show the photos to them before they left the airport for the trip home.

Mr. Isaacson was very excited to see the pictures.

"We are all very happy for you, son," he said. "Your bride and her parents really look nice." He paused before a photo of Rabbi and Rebbetzin Goldstein. "Really nice," he added.

"You will be coming to the wedding, won't you, Dad? You *must* come to the wedding."

His father laughed. "I haven't been overseas for years, and I was planning on one day taking the family on a trip. Perhaps we will make it in April. I can't give you a definite answer, son."

"Oh, Dad, you must come, you must."

Ari then went on to tell them all about Brocha, about his future parents-in-law, and about everything else that had happened over the last few weeks.

Yaakov gave an exaggerated sigh. "At least you have a new audience," he said. "I've been hearing about this every day," he laughed.

"We'll hear more about it in the morning," said Rabbi Levy as he dropped off Ari and his father. "I am sure both you boys need some rest, and so do we. It's nearly time to get up again."

Ari awoke with the sun streaming in through his window. He looked at his watch. What time was it? He gave a start. He had to be at *shul* right away. He washed, dressed quickly and was out of the house, wondering how on earth Sheila had managed to keep Debby and Yehudah from waking him. The house seemed to be empty. Sheila had obviously taken the children somewhere.

When he arrived back, he found a delicious breakfast waiting for him, with *hechsherim* on every item. Yehudah ran in straight after him and hugged him.

"Ari," he said. "Aren't I becoming a good cook? And Mummy bought all these cakes and rolls from the kosher bakery, and the cheese is *chalav Yisrael.* Zevi and I bought it."

"I'm impressed," said Ari. "It seems you manage to eat like a king over here."

"Not really," said Yehudah. "Sometimes I don't have anything really good for days and days. There are weeks in which Mum buys stuff for me, and other weeks where she gets all negative about it."

He suddenly stood back and shook Ari's hand firmly. "Oh, I forgot, *mazel tov*! I mean, I didn't really forget. I think about it all the time. But I forgot I hadn't said it to you."

"Where are Aunt Sheila and Debby?" asked Ari.

"Oh, my mother will be back soon," said Yehudah. "She just took Debby to ballet practice. There's a concert in three weeks time and it's going to be a big one, not just a children's one."

"Is she really such a good dancer?" asked Ari.

"Yes, she is. Or at least she reckons she is, and she is starting to have some solo parts in those adult shows, so I suppose she must be good. I haven't been to many of her concerts, though. They are mostly on Friday nights," he sighed.

"How's it going generally?" asked Ari. "I mean, with the *Yiddishkeit?*"

"As I say, it's good and bad," said Yehudah. "I'm trying very hard to get them to send me to the Yeshivah High School next year. At first I got an outright 'no', but sometimes I think they are yielding just a little. There are a few weeks left before term starts. If only they would let me! Zevi is going, of course." He looked somewhat despondent.

"*Shabbos* is difficult, too, all on my own. You aren't eating here tonight, are you?"

"No," said Ari, almost guiltily. He'd arranged to eat the *Shabbos* meals at the Levys.

"I'm used to it," said Yehudah dolefully. "But don't worry. You did it, and here you are marrying a rabbi's daughter. An important rabbi at that. I will do the same thing," he said, philosophically.

"Is there no way you can come with me to the Levys tonight?" asked Ari.

"No," said Yehudah. "I asked that already. There wasn't even a flicker of consent. No, I just have wait until I'm your age and can marry a rabbi's daughter and can have a kosher home."

"You don't have to marry a rabbi's daughter to have a kosher home!" said Ari vehemently.

They heard a car drive up, and within minutes, Sheila was in the house. Ari automatically stiffened, but then he remembered a conversation he had had with Brocha. He had told her all about Sheila, and about the conflicts they had had all through the years.

"Did you ever give her a chance?" Brocha had asked. "Here this woman marries your father and has two children, and then along comes a twelve-year-old boy, who resents her and hates her and refuses to respond to anything good she does."

He had to admit that he had never opened himself up to any kind of good relationship with his stepmother. Brocha was right. He promised he would try to do this. He felt a little nervous about it.

Here she was, arriving. Now was his chance. Wouldn't it be easier just to slide into the cool cordiality, peppered with aggressive comments and blown apart at times by blatant animosity? There was another way. He realized that now.

With this in mind, he greeted her with real warmth, and began to tell her all about Brocha and about his future parents-in-law. She was a little taken aback at first, and then began to respond. Even Yehudah was amazed at the way his brother was suddenly getting along with his mother. Here they were, chatting amicably. He hoped it would lessen, a little, her constant outbursts about him and about the havoc he had caused in the family.

"I'm trying to persuade your father that we should all go to England for the wedding," she was saying. "I've never been overseas before, and this would be a marvelous opportunity. Debby is longing to go as well so that we can audition her at the ballet academy and, of course, Jules just wants to go to the wedding. Then we could go across to France and Italy, and perhaps to Greece and Israel, and then fly back to Johannesburg."

"It sounds as though you really are coming," said Ari, delighted. "Dad seems so unsure."

"Don't worry," said Sheila. "You can be ninety percent sure that we will come. After all, how could he miss his oldest son's wedding?" she smiled.

"Oh, by the way, I bought some doughnuts from that kosher shop of yours. You'll need them for *Chanukah,* and I ate one on the way home. Delicious really, even though they are kosher," she added. "Actually, when you and Brocha come over, we will buy you some ready-made kosher chickens and give you paper plates and salads from a jar, and plastic knives and forks."

Yehudah was staring at his mother.

"Mum," he said. "Couldn't you get that for me for *Shabbos* and we could all eat it together, and we could start to have *Shabbos* just like they do in the Levy's house? Please, Mum. It would be so wonderful."

The atmosphere suddenly froze.

NINETEEN

It was late when Ari returned home from the *Shabbos* meal at the Levys. It was really good to be with them, almost like old times. They were thrilled to hear about Brocha and about the forthcoming wedding. Ari was hardly able to stop talking about it.

Mr. Isaacson opened the door for him.

"Anthony, I've been waiting up for you," he said. "I want to hear all about everything. Come, would you have some whiskey with me? Is it kosher? You can go and get one of your plastic cups."

They were soon sitting together drinking whiskey. Ari was telling his father about his *yeshivah* program, to his father's amazement.

"You work very hard, son, incredibly hard. How can you spend all those hours learning? Is it because this is required to enter the rabbinate?"

"No, Dad," said Ari, enjoying his father's concern. "We learn like that all the time over there."

"I didn't study like that for civil engineering," said his

father. "I mean, we had to work hard. Much more than the people who were doing arts degrees or anything like that. But you seem to work consistently, and what's more, you seem to love it."

They began to talk about Brocha and the wedding.

"Please, Dad, you must come, you really must. You're my father. I don't have anyone else. How can I get married without you?"

"You really feel that, Anthony?" questioned his father. "I thought that your mother turned you against me."

"That was long, long ago," said Ari. "She was bitter and upset because she lost you."

"I know," said his father. "I understand that. But it hurt when you stopped visiting me. You hardly wanted to speak to me on the phone."

"But, Dad," said Ari, "I didn't know you wanted me. I thought I was just a bother, a bother to whom you had to send money. The money was never enough, anyway. My mother and I had to struggle so much."

"Anthony," said Mr. Isaacson. "According to your mother's will, it seems that she didn't even spend all that I sent her. I know she had money from her mother's estate, but I'm sure it wasn't much. You were struggling so hard because she was always saving. She was always like that, even when we were married. She almost had an obsession with it. But of course, saving is good."

He looked affectionately at his son. "You have to learn these things, son, when you get married."

This led again to the subject of Brocha.

"I can't wait until you meet Brocha, Dad. You have never met such a wonderful girl."

"I saw your pictures from your engagement party," said his father. "She's a lovely girl, I can see. I hope we really get to know her as our own daughter-in-law."

"That's why you have to come to the wedding, Dad. I won't see her again until I'm in England, and then we'll be staying there for at least two years. Maybe forever."

Mr. Isaacson became very emotional. "You mean, in a way I will be losing you?" he said. "I know, son, that you have been away a lot, and we hardly saw you in the last three to four years, but I knew you were in South Africa. I knew that we could see one another if it was necessary. I knew you were still in the same country. But now you are going overseas. You will have children we will just know from photographs."

"But you must come and see us, Dad, and stay with us. And you must, you must come to the wedding."

"Tell me about a religious wedding," said his father. "I've heard it is very different from the normal ones we have in our synagogue."

"We have the *chuppah* outside, under the stars," said Ari.

"You don't really have dancing, do you?" said his father.

"We certainly do have dancing," said Ari. "It's different than what you're used to. We have separate dancing for men and women."

"That's odd," said his father. "Your mother and I did the waltz at our wedding. I mean, that was one of the main parts of the reception. How do you replace that?"

"We don't need to replace anything," said Ari. "We have so many unique Jewish practices that we don't need to adopt anyone else's customs."

"I was thinking about that," said his father. "I thought about it when you and Jules lit the *Chanukah* candles. Everyone around us is about to celebrate Xmas, and we always felt sort of left out. But then I realized that perhaps we had something also, and perhaps we don't need to make a special Xmas dinner to be the same as all the neighbors."

"Heaven forbid, Dad," said Ari. "Why should we want to celebrate their holiday?"

"It's just because everyone else does so," he finished lamely.

"Tell me about yours and Mum's wedding, my mother, that is," Ari asked. "How did you meet her? That is, if you don't mind talking about it. I never really asked because I couldn't. I mean, I didn't want to upset Aunt Sheila."

"I understand that," said his father. "I really loved your mother," he said. "She was really someone special, brilliant in her own way. Though she never had a chance to study because of Donald Levine." He pulled a face.

"Donald? Who is Donald?" asked Ari.

"You don't know?" asked his father, registering genuine surprise. "Oh, that was the man your mother was with before she met me."

"Oh, an old boyfriend," said Ari. "You mean you had to fight for her. He was your rival."

"No, no," said Mr. Isaacson. "He was long before I met her. But because of him, she didn't go to university. He was so insistent on marrying her."

"But she didn't," laughed Ari. "She waited for you to come along and sweep her off her feet."

"No, no," said his father, laughing at his son's teasing. "They did get married, but it was all over before I met her. The divorce was through at least a year before."

The color was beginning to drain from Ari's face. He felt he was beginning to faint. His heart pounded.

"And a *get*? Was there a *get*?" he whispered.

His father, a little overcome by whiskey and still responding to his son's teasing, continued: "To get a *get*? What do you mean, a *get*?" he laughed, a little giddy.

"I mean a Jewish divorce," said Ari.

"Oh, that! Oh, don't worry. I'm sure she didn't. Your mother bothering about what the rabbi said? Don't make me laugh. Who would bother about that, anyway? And Donald? That was never his style. Apparently he used to go to the beach on *Yom Kippur* and have a whale of a time because it was a holiday. He never darkened the doors of a *shul.* Don't worry, of course those two wouldn't get a *get.*

"Get a *get,*" he played with the words for a few minutes. "You certainly didn't inherit your religion from your mother, Anthony. She had no time for rabbis."

A wave of nausea overtook Ari. His head began to feel as if someone had put a tight steel band around it and was rapidly squeezing it shut. In those few moments he saw everything in his life vanishing around him as if an evil fire had consumed all his dreams, turning them to rotting ashes.

His father poured himself another drink. Suddenly he noticed that his son was looking very shocked and ill.

"What's the matter, son?" he asked. "Are you ill?"

Ari took a long time to answer. He raised his head from his hands and his father was shocked at the sight of his face. He was white, almost green, and his eyes were glassy. Eventually, Ari answered his father in a hoarse, strange voice.

"Dad, I might not be a kosher Jew," he said.

TWENTY

His father took a gulp of his whiskey, hardly aware that his own hand was shaking. Why was his son so white? Why did he look so ill and shocked? Was he not used to alcohol?

"I think you've been drinking too much, Anthony. I didn't realize you weren't used to it. Don't worry, you'll have a bit of a hangover in the morning, but in a day or two you will be right as rain. Maybe I can give you some of that medicine with vitamins in it. It's quite a good remedy, takes away the nausea."

Ari didn't respond, but eventually he repeated, as if in a trance:

"I might not be a kosher Jew."

"Anthony, of course you are kosher. You've been eating kosher for years. We know about that. We have been fighting with you about that. You were always very, very careful, and even though it drove us both round the bend, we still respected all your food fads. You've had too much to drink, that's all."

"Dad," said Ari, seeming to come back to himself a little, "it has nothing to do with food or whiskey. It's *me* that is all wrong."

"Don't be silly, Anthony. I didn't realize that the whiskey would put you into such a depressed, unreasonable state. When I find a depression coming over me, I resist it, fight it. I don't let it take hold."

"Dad," said Ari, "if my mother didn't have a *get*, I can't marry Brocha."

"What your mother did has nothing to do with you. Don't upset yourself about it. You just marry your Brocha and don't let anyone say you can't. You are just as good a Jew as anyone."

"No, Dad, I'm not, I'm not. If there was no *get*, I can't marry anyone . . . not really, anyway. There is no way I can marry Brocha."

"I don't understand you, Anthony," said his father. "Just because your mother made a failure of two marriages doesn't mean you have to judge yourself incapable of making a good one. You are very different than your mother, very, very different. Don't think that history has to repeat itself. Making a mess of a marriage doesn't have to go on to the next generation. We can learn . . ."

"It goes further than the next generation," said Ari. "It goes on forever."

"Anthony, stop saying such ridiculous things. You start your marriage afresh, and then you go on with it from there. Maybe you should see that psychologist again!"

"It won't help," said Ari, giving a groan from deep inside him, a groan which made his father shudder.

"Please Dad, try to remember. Are you sure there wasn't a *get*?" His mood suddenly lightened. "Dad, Mum never showed me wedding pictures."

"She destroyed them all."

"But weren't you married in a *shul*? A rabbi must have officiated."

"Anthony, I told you. Your mother hated rabbis. She didn't want to be married in a *shul*. We had a quiet ceremony in court with some friends as witnesses, and then we had a wonderful reception."

Ari once more sank into his state of shock and despair.

"Anthony," said his father, "I think all this is wedding nerves. I think we should all go to bed." He yawned and stumbled to his feet. "I'll talk to you in the morning, son. You'll feel much better then."

"Dad, I must talk to you now," said Ari, feeling he could not let his father sleep without giving him some kind of reassurance. "Dad, weren't there papers that Mum had about the first wedding? Didn't you see the marriage and the divorce papers? Didn't you need them for your own wedding?"

"Your mother organized all that," said his father, a little irritable that his son was keeping him away from his bed. "I suppose she had papers, but I think she lost them. You can find all that in the Population Register of Births, Deaths and Marriages. I'm going to bed, son."

"Dad, you can't leave me like this! You can't desert me. You've got to help me. Don't you understand? My whole world has gone, everything has gone. Dad, there's nothing left, there's no one left. Dad, I have no future! I have nothing. Dad, you've got to give me something, something to hold on to. Please, Dad, please help me! You've got to help me!" He started to sob and cry and his father tried to comfort him, saying that he should never again think of drinking whiskey. It obviously had a very bad effect on him.

"Dad," he began again, "Dad, maybe you saw a *get* or a

letter about a *get* somewhere in the house–a document, a Hebrew document. Maybe you saw it somewhere?"

"Anthony, I want you to go to bed, and I want to go to bed. I have to take your stepmother for the weekly shopping tomorrow. Anthony, you are acting in an impossible way. I haven't seen you as upset as this since . . . since the day you were in the hospital, when your Mum died!"

"Oh Mum, Mum!" Anthony began to wail. "Mum, why aren't you here now to answer my questions? Mum, how could you have done this to me? Mum, tell me you didn't do this to me!"

His father tried to get away, but Ari held onto him with both hands.

"Please Dad, don't go. Please Dad, tell me something. Tell me something! Give me something to take away the pain. Help me, Dad. You've got to talk to me!"

"Right, son," his father said. "I will help you. I didn't think this would affect you so much."

He stumbled out of the room and eventually returned with two tablets and a glass of water.

"I want you to take these with water, son. No more whiskey for you. I want you to take these and go to bed. They are fairly strong tranquilizers. They belong to Sheila. I have given you two. You will probably sleep until after lunchtime tomorrow. I am sure you need it. The rabbi won't mind. You can explain to him afterwards that you had a bad reaction to the whiskey and a very bad hangover and your father looked after you.

"I love you, son," he added, addressing the figure who seemed to have suddenly shrunk within himself.

He yawned. "I must go to bed. Got a hard day tomorrow. Your Aunt Sheila is impossible to shop with, and we need to replace some of our plants. The heat has really got to them.

We will spend a lot of time at the nurseries. It's been a difficult summer.

"Son, take these things and go to bed. Don't worry. We'll sort out everything in the morning. We all love you, Anthony."

With that, he was gone.

Twenty-One

Ari just sat, staring into space. His father had been a little drunk, that was quite obvious. But the information he had given could not have been imaginary. His mother had been married before and not had a *get*. He was a . . . he could not say the word, even to himself. The sheer horror of it made him want to fade into oblivion, to want to sink into the unknown, never to return.

But he could not just sit there. He had to do something. What? He had to speak to Yaakov.

He looked at the hall clock. It was two o'clock in the morning. Yaakov would be asleep. Or would he? He often stayed awake learning, especially on *Shabbos* evening. In *yeshivah* Ari had found him at three or four o'clock in the morning, unable to stop what he was learning, having become so absorbed in it. Perhaps there was a chance.

He slipped out of the house and ran through the darkened streets, aware that the sound of his shoes on the road was almost the only sound. He had walked and cycled so often down this road, he had known such joy, such happiness.

He tried to dry the tears as they persisted in falling, but eventually he gave up. Every time he wiped his hand across his eyes, his tears just fell faster. But who cared? What was there to care about any more? Was there any more meaning to his life? Why had he heard these things after he had met Brocha, after he had become engaged, after he had seen a whole glorious future ahead of him? Why couldn't he have heard these thing six months ago, when he would have just quietly dedicated himself to a solitary life of learning and community service?

Was it possible that he was not a kosher Jew? Perhaps that was why he found it difficult to concentrate in *davening*. Perhaps Hashem shut Himself off from him.

But that couldn't be. But was it? Why was he shown, as it were, the whole world ahead of him, and then had it snatched from him? Did he really have to pay the penalty for his mother's ignorance of Jewish law? The image of the framed snapshot of himself and his mother flashed through his mind, a ghostly reminder of a vanished time of trust and innocence.

He finally arrived at Yaakov's house. He knocked softly at the window. Yaakov appeared almost immediately. Even in darkness, he could see that Ari was greatly upset, and he went to the front door to let him in.

What could have happened? Ari looked like someone who hadn't slept or eaten for weeks, someone who had been shocked to his very being.

Yaakov saw that Ari had been crying. His eyes looked swollen and sore. Yaakov handed him some tissues and took him to his room.

"Ari, what's the matter? What can be the matter? What has happened? Has something dreadful happened to one of your family? Is Yehudah all right? Is your father all right?"

Ari nodded. He could not bring himself to speak. He just

allowed his tears to flow and cried, heartbroken.

"Ari," said Yaakov. "What can be wrong then? Ari, everything is going to be good. What is wrong?"

Ari said nothing. He just shook his head and continued to cry.

Yaakov let him cry for a few minutes. When it seemed that Ari was neither going to stop nor tell him what was the matter, he turned to his *sefer* and continued his learning in a soft, melodious voice.

The sound of the familiar words of Torah seemed to calm Ari. Slowly he stopped crying, and Yaakov turned to him.

As he looked at Ari, his own heart seemed to convulse as he saw his face. Yaakov had never seen anyone in such pain, even in the terminal wards of the hospital which he had visited with his father. His own eyes filled with tears.

"Ari, please tell me. Please, Ari. We are best friends, Ari. We have been for more than a decade."

"Not any more," said Ari. "You won't want to be my friend."

Yaakov frowned. "Why? What do you mean, Ari?" he asked.

"You will also reject me. You and your father will also look at me with contempt in the way that Brocha and the Goldsteins will." He started to sob again.

"Tell me what you're talking about, Ari. Would you rather speak to my father?"

"No," said Ari quickly. "No, your father must never know! I couldn't bear it. He trusted me so much."

"What have you done?" asked Yaakov.

"Nothing," said Ari.

"So why should he not trust you?"

"Because of who and what I am," said Ari.

"What are you talking about?" asked his friend. Was Ari

sick? Had he lost his mind? Was he imagining he was doing something really terrible?

"My mother never got a *get*," blurted out Ari.

Yaakov was puzzled.

"But that wouldn't affect you, Ari," he said. "It wouldn't even affect Yehudah and Debby. Aunt Sheila wasn't married before, was she?"

"No, she wasn't," said Ari. "Or, who knows? How can one know? How can one know when a woman has been married before?"

"But Ari?" began Yaakov, and then, as if a sword had gone right through him, he let the full impact of Ari's last words penetrate.

"Your mother was married before!" whispered Yaakov.

Ari nodded.

"You didn't know anything about that. I know you didn't. You heard tonight for the first time!"

Ari again nodded. He remained very still, waiting for the rejection he knew would follow.

"Ari, come let's say some *Tehillim*," said Yaakov. "We need our heads clear on this. We need the sweetness of Torah to give us some clarity. I don't believe it."

"It seems to be true," said Ari. "I asked my father over and over. Do you still want to learn with me?"

"Ari," said Yaakov, his own face white and his hands shaking. "We are going to search and find out that your mother had a *get*. But I want you to know something, and I'm sure I speak for my father, too. Ari, you are my best friend. You always will be my best friend. Even if you are, Heaven forbid, a . . ." he hesitated.

"Even if I'm not a kosher Jew," said Ari.

"Even, Heaven forbid," said Yaakov, "even if you are not as you say, a kosher Jew, you are my *chavrusah*, my friend, my best friend. I actually just read that even someone who is, as you say, not a kosher Jew, can still achieve greatness in Torah."

"Isn't such a person rejected by Hashem?"

"No, of course not. Though you have to speak to my father and definitely to Rabbi Weinstein about it. It is very important."

"I couldn't," said Ari. "How could I? Rabbi Weinstein made the *shidduch*. Oh, Yaakov, I can't marry Brocha! I can't marry anyone."

Yaakov said nothing.

"Come, let's say *Tehillim*," he said. "Let's get our minds and hearts back to where they should be."

"How can I say *Tehillim* now?" asked Ari. "I won't be able to concentrate. I can't even concentrate on *davening* any more. I knew something was wrong. It's because there is something wrong with me. My mind wanders all over the place during *davening*. I cover my eyes to say *Shema*, and I come back from my thoughts to realize I am right at the end of it and I haven't really concentrated on anything except the first line or two. And when I'm saying *Shemoneh Esrei* it's even worse than that. Maybe it's because I'm not a kosher Jew. I think that, perhaps, Hashem doesn't want to listen to my *davening*."

"Ari, Ari, that isn't true," said Yaakov. "That happens to every one on us."

"But if I knew Who I was *davening* to, I wouldn't let my mind wander. I mean, when I am talking to you, my mind doesn't wander. How can it wander when I'm talking to Hashem?"

"Ari, my father often said that if we knew Who we were *davening* to, or if we had only a fraction of an idea, we wouldn't be able to *daven* at all. We would be so overawed and overcome by the knowledge of it that we wouldn't be able to say one word. But everybody, absolutely everybody struggles with *davening*!"

Ari was crying again.

He looked up. "Yaakov," he said. "Brocha will be devastated. Just a few hours ago she was going to be mine, and now there is no way in heaven or on earth that I can ever marry her."

Twenty-Two

"Ari, let's say more *Tehillim*," said Yaakov gently. "Don't think about Brocha now. You can't do that. I know how it must be hurting you. Come, learn with me for twenty minutes and then we will discuss a plan of action."

"Action?" said Ari.

"Yes, of course," said Yaakov. "We have to do something, but let's learn a little first. Then our thoughts will be a bit more settled."

Even through his shock and grief, Ari felt a certain relief in the words of *Tehillim*. It was as if he had something to hold onto, something which was permanent, something which couldn't be taken away from him. They said *Tehillim* for longer than they had planned, but Ari felt, when they had finished, that he could in fact plan some action, a thing which he had felt incapable of doing before.

"On *Shabbos* we can't make definite plans," said Yaakov. "But we can get an idea of what we can do. You have to speak to a *rav*."

"I can't," said Ari. "I can't bear to speak to one. It will make things so definite."

"Maybe it won't," said Yaakov. "We know in general where you stand, if your mother didn't get a *get*. But maybe there are other factors to take into account. We have to speak to a *rav*, someone familiar with the whole subject. Unfortunately, you can't possibly be the first person in the *yeshivah* world who has had this problem."

"We know the situation," said Ari. "It's a total disaster. I am a blemished person, and I can't marry someone who is born Jewish unless they themselves have the same problem. And I can't marry Brocha." His tears began to well up and he cried. "I don't know what I am going to do. My mind is just exploding. I can't take it, Yaakov, I can't."

"Please speak to my father," said Yaakov.

"No," said Ari, "I can't. I just can't."

"Then you should go back to Johannesburg as soon as possible, tomorrow night even, if you can get a plane. You have got to speak to Rabbi Weinstein."

"I know I have to do that," said Ari finding it difficult to speak through his tears. "I know that I have to speak to him because of . . . because of the *shidduch*. But I can't."

"What else can you do?" asked Yaakov. "What option do you have?"

"You are right," said Ari. "I will try."

"There's another thing," said Yaakov. "How does your father know absolutely that your mother didn't have a *get*? I mean, he didn't ask for one. The question of being married in a *shul* didn't seem to have been raised. How would he know?"

"I don't want to think about that," said Ari. "I don't want to think positively, because I can't bear to hope. It will just be more difficult to accept when it comes to nothing."

"I understand," said Yaakov. "But we have to do research. We have to investigate. We have to find your mother's relatives and ask them. They will be able to help us, I am sure. How about your aunts, uncles and cousins?"

"I don't know any of her relatives. I don't have any aunts or uncles on my mother's side, not that I know of anyway," said Ari wearily.

"What was your mother's maiden name?"

"Shapiro," said Ari.

"You surely must be able to find out something," said Yaakov.

"But Yaakov," said Ari, tears starting to flow again. "It might take months and months to learn anything, and by that time, I would have lost everything!"

Yaakov had to agree that that was true.

For a few minutes there was silence between them. Yaakov stifled a yawn.

"It's late," said Ari. "You need to go to bed. I am sorry I kept you up for so long. It must be nearly morning."

"I am tired, yes," said Yaakov. "But you mustn't be sorry you kept me up so long. We had to talk about this, and I don't think either of us will sleep well for the rest of the night, anyway."

"Yaakov, what am I going to do? What am I going to do?" asked Ari. "Everything is going. Everything has gone."

"Speak to Rabbi Weinstein," said Yaakov. "Go to him as soon as possible. He will know what to do. Go back tomorrow night, if you can."

Ari left Yaakov and walked home slowly. He had made certain that Yaakov had given his word that the situation would remain a secret. It was dark, very dark. Rabbi Levy had always said that the darkest hour was before the dawn.

This felt like his darkest hour, but this time there was no

dawn. Life would become a never-ending tunnel of darkness.

He did not try to hold back the tears. He couldn't. They would just have to fall unchecked. Oh, why had his father mentioned Donald Levine? He would have been married and then . . . no! He couldn't think that way. Hashem had made the world, and it was Hashem's Torah. If there had been such a flaw in his birth, he could not marry Brocha. He just had to thank Hashem that he found out before it was too late. But he found this difficult. It was something he had to work on.

He knew he should see Rabbi Weinstein. He knew he had no option. And suddenly he knew he had to speak to him as quickly as possible and then leave Johannesburg, leave South Africa and go and learn in some far-off *yeshivah*, of course, nowhere near England. He shuddered as he thought of the expressions of horror which would be on Rabbi and Rebbetzin Goldstein's faces, and their thankfulness that their daughter had been saved from such a catastrophic marriage.

Surely there were other people, other *frum* Jews who had been *baalei teshuvah*, or whose parents had been, who had faced this problem. What was the solution? They couldn't marry into the congregation of Israel. But they could, perhaps, marry one another, and their children could marry one another. He wondered if there would be a select group of Jews who knew that they could intermarry only among themselves.

But he must not go on mind trips. He was exhausted. As his house came into view, he slipped inside, and very shortly afterwards, was asleep.

He awoke later than he had intended, and realized that he would have to hurry to *shul*.

Yehudah greeted him and then looked at him hard.

"Ari, what's the matter?" he said, frowning. "Ari, you look

sick. Are you all right?"

"Yehudah, I have the most terrible headache," said Ari, not untruthfully.

"I can see that," said Yehudah. "Your eyes are all red and swollen, and you have dark rings underneath them."

"Yehudah," said Ari. "I might have to leave straight after *Shabbos*. There is something I have to do in Johannesburg."

His brother looked disappointed.

"Oh Ari," he said, "I so wanted you to be here. There is so much I wanted to talk to you about."

"Another time," said Ari. "Maybe this afternoon if I am feeling better."

Yehudah nodded, somewhat satisfied.

"I must hurry to go to *shul*," said Ari. "I don't want to be too late."

He felt he could not talk to Yehudah, he just had nothing to give, nothing at all. And, who was he to give it, anyway?

He could not keep back the tears during the *davening*, though he tried to be as unnoticed as possible, announcing as he walked in that he had a dreadful sinusitis attack. He was too exhausted and dejected to really care however. He *davened* almost mechanically, suddenly realizing that up to that point, even though he had lost concentration at times, his *davening* had in fact been alive and meaningful. Now he felt like a computer simply acting the way he had been programmed, feeling nothing except the fierce pain in his chest and heart.

He was invited for lunch at the Levys, and he tried to keep himself together so that they could not see how upset he was. He did explain again about his terrible sinusitis attack. Were they convinced? He didn't know. All he knew was that Rabbi Levy had given him a look of compassion and understanding which seemed to soothe his soul a little.

But surely Rabbi Levy didn't know what was troubling him. Yaakov would never have told him. Somehow, he sensed that something was very, very wrong.

Rabbi Levy indeed knew that something was wrong, and that Yaakov would tell him nothing about it. He was not deceived by Yaakov's white, strained face and the dark rings under his eyes which almost matched Ari's. He decided, then, that he would say *Tehillim* for Ari. Even though he didn't know what was troubling him, Hashem knew.

Neither Ari nor Yaakov ate much at the *Shabbos* meal, and directly after it was over, they learned together. Ari then went home.

Yehudah wanted to speak to him, and he asked him to come into his room. Ari said that he was just going to lie down a little and would speak to him afterwards.

He awoke two hours later and called Yehudah to him, but he could see the boy was upset. He asked him what was troubling him.

"You were crying in your sleep, Ari," he said. "You were groaning and crying as if you had heard something terrible or lost someone. I was frightened."

"It was a bad dream," said Ari, "a nightmare. Or, shouldn't I say, a 'daymare'."

The boy smiled hesitantly.

"It was just my headache," said Ari. "My head was sore, over here." He pointed to his forehead.

"Is that all?" asked Yehudah.

"That's all," said Ari.

There was, in fact, space on the midnight flight back to Johannesburg that *Motzei Shabbos*. Immediately after *Shabbos*, after lighting the *Chanukah licht* and waiting the appropriate time, Ari packed his suitcase, explaining to his parents that something had come up and he had to be in Johannesburg right away.

They too, had not been fooled. They realized that something was terribly wrong, and Mr. Isaacson could not really understand what it was. He knew it had something to do with their conversation the previous night, and of course, the whiskey, but that conversation was somewhat hazy to him. What had they really talked about? Only the past and the future. Was this a mixture of whiskey and wedding nerves? He hoped his son wasn't going to back out of the wedding now. It would hardly be fair to the girl. But he said nothing.

Yaakov fetched Ari in his father's car and drove him to the airport. Both knew that he had to speak to Rabbi Weinstein as soon as possible.

They hardly spoke in the car. Neither knew what to say, apart from the fact that they were both exhausted.

"Don't wait for me to get on the plane," said Ari. "You really look tired. I'll be all right. I will see you in *yeshivah* when you arrive on Tuesday. Don't worry. I'll survive until then!"

Yaakov nodded. He was really tired, and his head ached.

"Yaakov," said Ari, "you gave your word not to tell anybody."

"That's right," said Yaakov.

"Thanks," said Ari. "See you Tuesday . . ."

Twenty-Three

It was with some trepidation that Yaakov approached the *yeshivah* dorm that Tuesday morning. He had not heard from Ari since he had left him at the airport on *Motzei Shabbos*, and he had half expected him to phone after he had spoken to Rabbi Weinstein.

He wondered what the rabbi had said and what Ari was feeling. Well, he would soon find out.

Yaakov was still shocked by Ari's situation. He had found difficulty in eating and sleeping, and he had gone around with a sick, anxious feeling inside. If only Rabbi Weinstein could do something about it, or if only they could find some evidence that there was a *get*.

But he would have heard from Ari if there had been any good news, he was sure.

It had been difficult not to confide in his father, but of course, there was no way he could possibly do it. He was well aware, though, that his father knew there was something wrong and was extremely concerned. However, he did not even try to question Yaakov, knowing somehow that he had given his word to secrecy.

"Hi, Yaakov. How was Cape Town?" He saw Yerachmiel approaching. He was about to respond as cheerfully as he could when the *bachur's* next few words sent his head reeling.

"When is Ari coming back? Is he staying a few more days with his family?"

Yaakov said nothing and just nodded, taking his suitcases into his room. He needed time to think. Had Ari in fact not arrived? Where was he? There was no way that Yerachmiel could not have seen him. The *bachurim* spent all their time together.

He sat on the bed and put his head in his hands. He was becoming sick, sick with worry over his friend. Where, oh where was Ari?

Perhaps he had come quietly to the *yeshivah* and spoken to Rabbi Weinstein and then gone off somewhere, or perhaps he had gone to the Weinstein's home, spoken to him and then left. But surely he would have phoned and told him, or left some kind of note.

Without unpacking anything, he walked along the passage to Ari's room and, out of habit, knocked softly at the door before he opened it and went in.

There was no sign that Ari had been back to the *yeshivah* at all.

He groaned as he saw a photograph from the engagement party on Ari's bedside table. He picked it up and looked into the happy and excited faces of Ari and Brocha and her mother and father. Without even thinking, he turned the photo face downwards as he put it back.

Ari definitely had not been back. He would never had left the photograph there.

If even he, Yaakov, couldn't bear to look at the picture, how could Ari have done it? There were also other things from the *vort* all around the room, a piece of ribbon, a *bentcher*, a few tiny plastic glasses they had used to make *l'chaim*.

He quickly went out and shut the door. The room was too full of joy and expectations for the future. He could not bear to be there.

He turned once more towards his room and saw Reuven coming towards him.

"I see your *chavrusah* isn't here yet. When is he coming?"

"Oh, in a few days," said Yaakov. What else could he say? Oh, where was Ari? He was not in Cape Town, he himself had been there for the last few days. There was no way he could not have seen him, no way at all. And he himself had taken Ari to the airport on that *Motzei Shabbos*.

But he also was not in the *yeshivah*. Where else could he be?

Perhaps he should ask Rabbi Weinstein if Ari had spoken to him. But what if Ari hadn't come to the *yeshivah* at all? Rabbi Weinstein knew that Ari and Yaakov were in Cape Town together, and he would assume that Ari was still with his parents. Asking him would only confuse matters.

What could he do without making the situation worse? He was beginning to feel very desperate.

Perhaps Ari had not wanted to face things alone. Perhaps he wanted to wait until Yaakov was with him before he approached Rabbi Weinstein.

Yaakov settled down a little. Ari would probably come today. Yaakov had not known which plane he was coming on. Ari hadn't known himself. He could be back in the evening, or at the latest tomorrow.

With that uneasy reassurance, Yaakov found he could carry on with what he had to do.

He would go into the *yeshivah* hall and learn.

If he had looked for any length of time in a mirror, Yaakov would have realized that he did not look well at all. He was several shades paler than usual and his eyes had dark rings under them.

As soon as Rabbi Weinstein saw him, he realized that something was wrong, desperately wrong, but he did not want to ask directly. Was Yaakov not well?

"Welcome back to the *yeshivah*, Yaakov," he said, shaking his hand. "How are you?"

"*Baruch Hashem*," said Yaakov.

A feeling of uneasiness stirred inside the rabbi. What was wrong?

"How's Ari? When is he coming back?" he asked.

He did not miss a flicker of fear passing across Yaakov's eyes.

"Ari will be here in a few days," Yaakov said. "He is with his family."

He wasn't a person who could lie easily, and the words seemed to come out all wrong. The rabbi was not deceived.

"Something is wrong, Yaakov," he said. "I can see it written all over your face. What is wrong?"

"Nothing, Rabbi Weinstein, nothing is wrong," said Yaakov, wishing with all his heart that he could have confided in the rabbi.

"Is everybody well? Is Ari well?" he said.

"Yes, yes of course," said Yaakov. "Everyone is well, *Baruch Hashem*."

"When is Ari coming back?" repeated the Rabbi.

"In a few days' time," said Yaakov, knowing he was sounding vague. He wished the rabbi would stop questioning him. He hated having to lie. Oh where, oh where was Ari?

"How did your few days of holiday go?" asked the rabbi.

"*Baruch Hashem*," answered Yaakov.

"Please Yaakov, I must know what is wrong. Whatever it is, Yaakov, you can trust me. Please tell me," said the rabbi.

Yaakov shook his head.

"I can't tell you, Rabbi Weinstein," he said at last. "I wish I could tell you, but I can't. I gave my word that I wouldn't."

Yaakov went over to his table and took out his *Gemara*. This was sanity, this was real, this was life itself. He wondered if Ari, wherever he was, was also learning. Surely he would be. Wherever he was, he had a few of his *sefarim* and his *Chanukah licht*. How could he have disappeared? He forced himself to concentrate on the *sefer* in front of him.

Rabbi Weinstein watched him, the feeling of unease growing inside of him. What could be wrong with Ari? Was he doubting the *shidduch*?

But the boy had been so happy. This was what he had wanted, the rabbi knew that. He and Brocha had seemed so suited, so beautifully matched in every way. They had both sparkled since they had met one another. That surely had not changed.

No, something else was wrong. What could it be? Yaakov obviously knew, but could not tell him. The rabbi knew that he longed to tell him. He could see in Yaakov's eyes that he was desperate to discuss it with him.

He also did not seem to know when Ari was returning to the *yeshivah*.

He would have to find out for himself. He would give it a few hours, and then contact Cape Town.

Twenty-Four

M*otzei Shabbos*, after Yaakov dropped him off at the airport, Ari stared at the screen listing the departure times. He still had forty minutes before the plane took off. As he watched, however, the figures on the board started to change as the flight was rescheduled two hours later. That made two hours and forty minutes.

He sat on one of the chairs, overcome by exhaustion and numbness. Life, for him, had come to a halt. He had no future. He had cried so much that he felt as if his tears had dried up, leaving a dull, aching, nauseating emptiness.

Two hours and forty minutes. What could he do in that time? He wouldn't arrive in *yeshivah* until morning. Another night with no sleep. Well, though every bone in his body ached for it, sleep, he felt, would not be his companion for a long time. And then, he would have to face the *yeshivah* and Rabbi Weinstein.

How could he? What if the rabbi changed towards him, which of course he could. His outstanding *bachur* would now be simply an unkosher Jew who would not be welcome, he was sure, in the *yeshivah.*

He could picture the rabbi's face fill with horror at the thought of what he had nearly brought about in a *shidduch.* He would rush out and phone his friend, Rabbi Goldstein, to cancel it all. How could he face him?

He got up and began to pace the airport, keeping an eye on his luggage. How long would he do this for? His legs felt heavy as he dragged his feet after him. Was this the person who had been in the *yeshivah* athletic team?

No, it wasn't. That had been, or he thought he had been, a kosher Jew. This was simply a . . . He could not bear to think about it.

If only he could disappear, or run away or evaporate. But where could he run to? There was nowhere.

He looked back at the departure times on the board. There was another midnight flight, and this one was right on schedule. The only problem was that this one was going to Durban. Problem? Maybe this was the answer. He would change his ticket for Durban, stay there until Tuesday, and then join Yaakov at the *yeshivah.* Perhaps he would feel better about talking to Rabbi Weinstein when Yaakov was around.

Almost as if in a dream, he walked over to the ticket office.

Once he was already in the air, Ari started having second thoughts about what he was doing. Why was he going to Durban? He hadn't been there for years and years. Who was he going to? Stephen? To Mrs. McNeally? Was he going to the Addington Hospital to search the casualty department for some remembrance of his mother? Did he want to find the social worker? Why was he travelling to Durban instead of to Johannesburg?

A wave of depression came over him, different in quality from his shock and grief. As he felt its familiar shadow, he realized he hadn't felt this feeling for months, in some ways, years. Now the emptiness, the hollowness, the blackness, was beginning to creep up on him. Did it matter where he was going? Did it matter any more if he went to Johannesburg or Durban or Bloemfontein or anywhere else? Did life have any meaning for him any more?

Rabbi Levy's words started to filter through to him. There were thoughts he could not afford to entertain. They would, he knew, lead him to despair and hopelessness, and he would not be able to function. He could not afford this. He had to keep himself together. He was going to Durban to spend two days on his own so that he could have time to think. No one would miss him in the *yeshivah*. No one knew he was coming.

Yaakov wouldn't be there until Tuesday. He would be back by then.

It seemed strange to see the lights of Durban City. Why was he landing here? And yet the lights seemed to draw him towards the city. He had to go again to see everything, to see Addington Hospital, to see the hotel he had stayed in with his father, to walk on the beach and play the computer games.

Was he reverting to childhood? Was he losing his mind? No, what he felt and had been feeling now was almost the same as what he had been feeling then: the same sense of desolation and desperation, as if everything had left him in one cruel moment.

He started to feel the pain again, and he tried to shut his mind against it and reached for his overnight bag on the rack above him.

It was very early morning, not much past one-thirty. He would remain in the airport until daybreak and take a light aircraft or even a railway bus to Margate, close to his old home.

He felt in his pocket for his Autobank card. He would need to draw more money from his account. But he would do that later.

He collected his luggage and found some comfortable seats at the far end of the airport. He would learn for a while, but first he would shut his eyes for a few minutes.

"The SAA Flight 212 from London is now landing."

Ari awoke with a start. What time was it? How long had he been asleep, and why had that broadcast of all the announcements he had heard through the night, woken him?

SAA from London. He would have been taking SAA to London, if only this mess hadn't happened. His despair latched ruthlessly onto his brain and to his body. Would it never leave him? Where, oh where would there ever be any peace for him in the world? He found a place to wash and then to *daven.*

He must find out about the plane to Margate. He would be able to find a room there, he was sure. Even mid-season there were always rooms to rent at the seaside resort.

But years had passed, the holiday makers had increased, and it took him two hours to find a room. It was at quite a distance from the sea, on the inland side of the South Coast Road. The room was not in Margate itself, but further down the coast, in fact, fairly near to his old home. He had seen in those two hours that Margate had changed considerably. The curio shop did not seem to be there anymore. In its place there was a large hotel.

He put his luggage into the room and went outside to walk the two kilometers to his old apartment.

How strange it was to once more be walking along the paths he knew so well. True, the town had changed and become more built up, but the core was still there. The popular beaches had become more populated, but the rugged and rocky coastal areas were still the same. Memories from the past began filtering in, and eventually flooded into his mind.

He looked at the warm, radiantly blue waters of the Indian ocean and the lush evergreen foliage. He had almost forgotten its beauty and the sunshine of the South Coast of Natal.

His old apartment was still there, though the building had aged and weathered somewhat. Now there was a security door on the front of the building and buttons with the name of each occupant. He looked at number six, his old home. A Becker family lived there. Should he ring the buzzer and ask if he could see it?

He was standing uncertainly near the buttons when he caught sight of the name opposite number 1. Mrs. McNeally. Was she still there? Was she still the caretaker?

Without thinking further he rang the buzzer. Mrs. McNeally's voice came through the speaker, "Yes?"

"It's Ari, Anthony, Anthony Isaacson."

"Anthony!" The security gate buzzed and he pushed it and was quickly being ushered into Mrs. McNeally's apartment.

"Anthony, I wouldn't have recognized you except that you look so much like your father. Remember when he came over here with you after your dear mother died? I suppose he looks older now. And of course, you have a beard. In fact, you look like a rabbi. Are you a rabbi?"

The old lady turned to him in wonderment.

"I am studying to be one," began Ari, and then he stopped. Could he still be a rabbi? Surely not. How could a person with a smear on his birth become a rabbi? But he must not think about that.

He sat down at her invitation, declining the food offered him.

"Please tell me all your news," she said. "Are you married yet, or engaged?"

A look of such sorrow crossed his face that even Mrs. McNeally couldn't miss it.

"A broken heart," she said. "You loved someone and it didn't work out, and now you have a broken heart."

He smiled. "Yes," he said, "Yes, that is it exactly."

"It is hard," she said. "It is very, very hard. It takes time to get over it. What was her name?"

"Brocha," said Ari, wondering why he was telling her all this.

"Maybe it will still work out," she said. "You never know. Sometimes something happens, and it all comes right. Isn't that possible?"

"Not this time, I don't think so," he said.

"Another man, heh? Though I don't know how she could leave you for him. Quite a handsome fellow you've grown into," she murmured sympathetically.

"Mrs. McNeally," said Ari, feeling the conversation was becoming far too personal for his liking, "would it be possible for me to see my old flat? I just want to see it again. I think about it so often. Shall I ask the Beckers? I see they are the new occupants?"

"Oh, they are away at work," said the woman. "They both work in Port Shepstone. They won't be home until after six o'clock this evening."

He was disappointed.

"But I have the key," she went on. "I have the keys to all the apartments. If you promise not to tell anyone, I will take you up there myself . . . just for a few minutes, mind you."

He felt a sob catch at his throat as he saw the apartment.

It had different furnishings, of course, but this was the apartment he had shared with his mother for many years. He walked into the tiny kitchen. Even the stove was the same. Did it still work? How could it still be working?

They spent at least fifteen minutes in the apartment, Mrs. McNeally not wanting to break the almost trancelike way in which Ari looked at everything. He spent some time at the window and when he turned around again, she saw that his eyes were suspiciously red. Brocha must have been a lovely girl, or was it his mother he was missing, or both?

He suddenly walked towards the door. "Let's go back to your apartment," he said. "I've finished here."

He followed her quickly down the stairs, and once more sat with her in her lounge.

She tried to offer him coffee and eventually realized he wouldn't eat her food.

"What about a Coke in a can?" she said.

"That would be fine," he replied. He was getting somewhat thirsty.

"What made you become so religious?" she asked. "Your mother wasn't religious, and your father didn't look religious, though you never know."

She seemed to get an idea. "That's it!" she said. "Maybe your Brocha found you too religious, too serious. Maybe you should lighten up a bit, shave off that beard and put on some jeans. Then that other guy wouldn't have a hope against you."

He smiled.

"Maybe I should come shopping with you. You could get some really way-out T-Shirts."

"It's all right," he said, gently. "Thanks anyway. Tell me what is new with you," he continued.

She told him all about her family, about her cousin who had won a fortune at Sun City, about her nephew who had gone to university and done very well, and about her husband who had passed away two years ago.

"I'm sorry," he said.

She was silent and then said, "You see, I do understand how you feel."

"Thanks," he said. Oh, why was there so much suffering!

"Are you . . . are you all right now?" he asked.

"It takes time," she said. "At first I was numb, and then I cried all the time. But as time goes on, it comes in waves and the waves are often not so bad, and they are fewer and further apart. But it still hurts."

"I know," he whispered. "It was like that when Mum died."

There was silence between them and then he spoke.

"Did you know my mother before she came to this apartment?" he asked.

"Before you two came together, after the divorce? No," she replied.

"Do you know anyone who knew her before?" he asked.

"I don't think so," she said. "It is so long ago. But Anthony, don't try to relive and revive the past. It doesn't work."

He left the apartment building saying he would contact her again, and took the path to the ocean. He knew this to be a deserted part of the coast. No one went there. Even the fishermen avoided it. As a child, it had been a favorite haunt. He had even persuaded his mother to come with him at times.

Being in the apartment had sharpened his memories of his mother. He loved her, and yet, what had she done to him? By not getting a *get* she had ruined his future, ruined his life. He suddenly felt angry with her. Why had she not been careful of his Jewish heritage? Why had she not found out what was necessary to make her children kosher Jews? Why did he have to find out at this stage that she had, according to *halachah*, not been a mother fit to have a child?

But his anger did not last long. He thought about her and everything within him clamored to excuse her. She did not know, or if she did know, she had no idea of the importance of a *get*. It must have been out of ignorance rather than carelessness. But it could have been so easy, so very, very easy.

She had always given him the best of everything. She had been careful of his schooling, had given him extra lessons. She had given him all his injections and everything necessary to protect him against all kinds of things. She had even insisted on orthodontic treatment (which his father had paid for). Why had she not taken care that her son would be fit to be allowed to marry another Jew? Didn't she know that the position was irreversible?

He started to cry, hot tears which rolled down his cheeks and splashed onto the sand and the rocks. He could cry freely now with only the sea to witness it, and what if gallons of salty tears mingled with the sea? He felt that they would never stop, and indeed he could not have stopped them.

"Mum, why did you do this to me? Why did you do this? Mum, you loved me, but even you couldn't reverse it. From the moment I was conceived, it was too late!" And then, his tears still flowing freely, he said, "Mum, if there is a *get*, anywhere in the world, show me where it is. Show me how to find it! But there isn't Mum, is there? How can there be?"

He walked back to his room and lay in his bed. He was tired, very tired. His head ached and his eyes and his throat were swollen from crying. He didn't feel well. He *davened Maariv* and fell asleep. He didn't feel well at all.

He awoke sometime during the night, shivering and

weak. He staggered over to his table and set out the *menorah*. Why were his hands trembling so much when he lit it? And yet, the flames seemed to comfort him a little, as if he could find some kind of refuge within them.

He had felt the same about *davening* and the little learning he had managed to do. It had become a haven for him to go to, a city of refuge.

But he was weak, very weak and he returned to his bed after taking a few bites of the *matzoh* he had bought from the corner store. That, and water and some fruit was what he had decided to live on, and indeed, he had no option for the next few days, because his temperature shot up and wouldn't come down. He lay in a half delirium, rising at times to *daven* a few words before he would once again fall, shivering and confused, onto his bed.

Twenty-Five

By late Tuesday night, Rabbi Weinstein felt he had to make his own investigations. There had been no sign of Ari, and Yaakov's agitation was becoming progressively undisguised. Rabbi Weinstein decided to phone Rabbi Levy, Yaakov's father, and ask him what was troubling the boys.

He felt even more concerned after the call. Rabbi Levy had thought Ari was in Johannesburg. He definitely wasn't in Cape Town. Yaakov himself had driven him to the airport to catch the midnight plane on *Motzei Shabbos.*

According to Rabbi Levy, both boys had been upset, but had refused to tell him anything about it. He gathered that Yaakov had given his word to say nothing. Something was definitely disturbing Ari very, very deeply.

Ari had apparently been fine and happy at the *Shabbos* meal on Friday night, but then he had gone home and returned quite some time later and spoken to Yaakov far into the night.

The next day he had looked like someone in severe

emotional and spiritual pain and had left, apparently for Johannesburg, as soon as possible.

"There is something wrong," said Rabbi Levy, "something very wrong. I have never seen Ari like this, even when I first met him shortly after his mother died."

Both rabbis had surmised that something had obviously disturbed Ari at home. Could he phone his father? The boy was neither in Cape Town nor in the *yeshivah* in Johannesburg. He was missing. This was an emergency.

Rabbi Weinstein dialed the Isaacson's number.

A somewhat irritable Mr. Isaacson answered, "Yes?" he said. "What time is it? Who wants to speak to me?"

"It is Rabbi Weinstein, from Johannesburg. Your son seems to be missing."

There was silence for a few minutes.

"Missing. Anthony? But he has been with you since early Sunday morning. He said he had to fix up something urgently. When did he become missing?"

"He never arrived here," said Rabbi Weinstein.

"Why didn't you tell us before? Why did you wait until Tuesday?" he demanded.

"I only knew a short while ago," said the rabbi. "I thought he was still in Cape Town."

"But where is he?" asked Mr. Isaacson.

The rabbi did not answer. Instead, he asked, "Was he upset about something?" he asked.

"No, he was very excited . . . but . . . wait a minute. He was rather upset on Friday night. It was the whiskey!"

"Whiskey?" asked the rabbi.

"Yes," said his father. "The whiskey made him upset."

"What happened?" asked the rabbi.

"Well, I must try to remember," he said. "I was drinking whiskey too. I didn't realize he wasn't used to drinking, and he felt very sick. He was still feeling sick the next day, and then you wanted him urgently in Johannesburg, so he left to speak to you."

It was still very confusing.

"You and Ari, I mean, Anthony, were drinking together?" asked the *rosh yeshivah.*

"Well, we don't do it usually, but I thought we needed to talk man to man. I mean, he is going to be married soon. We are all very excited about it." He continued, "We spoke for a long time and then the whiskey got to him, and he got very sick."

"What were you talking about?" asked the rabbi.

"Oh, about old times, about his mother, about our first meeting. He seemed upset when I mentioned Donald Levine. He had never heard about him before."

"Who is that?" asked the rabbi, his hand began to shake.

"Oh, his mother's first husband. They were married for a very, very short time, nothing really in it. No children or anything. It just didn't work out."

Rabbi Weinstein felt his mouth go dry and his heart began to beat faster. He had difficulty catching his breath.

"Was there a *get*?" he asked.

"Oh, that was it. That is what Anthony latched on to. He kept asking if there was a *get*, and I said no, of course there wasn't. She wasn't the type of woman to chase around looking for a *get* when you can get a perfectly good legal divorce. I don't know why he went on about it so much. Got the 'marble' he did. The whiskey got him that way. Started to say his life was ruined, his future was ruined and he could not marry Brocha. Quite weird he was that night, rattled me rather and rattled the whole family the next day. Jules was very upset. Anthony looked quite sick, and he had a massive hangover."

"His life had been shattered," said the rabbi.

"What do you mean?" asked Mr. Isaacson. "What did I do to him?"

Calmly he explained the situation to the father. He also explained the potential gravity of the situation.

"You mean," Mr. Isaacson said, beginning to sound really horrified, "you mean that by marrying me without a *get*, my ex-wife was not properly divorced? Our marriage was not proper, and that makes my son a . . ."

"Yes," said the rabbi, his own voice full of pain. "If your ex-wife didn't have a *get*, Ari would not, Heaven forbid, be a kosher Jew, to use a euphemism."

"But his mother is dead now, so it all cancels out, doesn't it?"

"Unfortunately not," said the rabbi. "In fact, once the child is conceived, nothing cancels it."

"You mean it is irreversible? But nothing is irreversible. The rabbi said on *Yom Kippur* that one could repent for anything."

"If one, Heaven forbid, killed a person and repents, would the person come alive?"

"No, of course not," said Ari's father. "Yes, I get what you mean. Now what must we do about it?"

"We have to investigate the situation thoroughly," said the rabbi. "If there was a *halachically* kosher marriage to Donald Levine, and if there was no *get* before she married you, there is probably very little we can do."

"You mean, it stays that way? Can Anthony really not marry Brocha?"

"If that is the case, that's what it is all about."

"I have to speak to someone about this," said Mr. Isaacson. "I'll speak to Rabbi Levy first thing tomorrow. It can't really be like this. We must do something to fix it up, Rabbi

Weinstein." His voice was full of emotion. "Please help us do something about this. You have to help us. We didn't know!"

"Have you any idea where Ari could be?" asked the rabbi, changing the subject.

"He's really not with you?" asked Mr. Isaacson.

"I haven't seen him since he left for Cape Town," said the rabbi. "Could he still be there?"

"I doubt it," said his father. "Where would he go?" He was silent for several seconds.

"Didn't Yaakov see him catch the plane to Johannesburg?" he asked at last.

"I haven't been able to speak to him. I will do so now," said the rabbi.

"Please call me back," said Ari's father. "I have to know what is happening. You don't . . . you don't think he has done anything, anything silly, I mean . . ."

"I don't think so," said the rabbi, still feeling sick from the whole situation. He suddenly realized that Mr. Isaacson was sniffing rather a lot and his voice sounded choked up.

"Rabbi," he said, "you have to help us. I didn't know, otherwise I would have insisted on a *get*. I will go anywhere, do anything to get this thing fixed up."

Mr. Isaacson was about to put the phone down when he had an idea. "Could he have gone to Durban?" he asked. "He and his mother used to live on the South Coast."

"I will speak to Yaakov," said the rabbi. "I'll find out if he *saw* him actually catch the plane."

"Phone me," said the boy's father. "I can't go to sleep until I hear from you. Please phone me back."

Yaakov sat in his room, his head in his hands. What, oh what was he to do? Where was Ari? He had to do something, tell someone, but he had given his word he would tell no one.

But what if something had happened to Ari?

There was a knock at the door and he called for the person to come in. He stood up quickly when he saw it was Rabbi Weinstein. Why did the rabbi look so pale? Had he had news that something had happened to Ari?

He began to apologize for not going to the door.

"It's nothing," said the rabbi. "I have just been speaking to Ari's father."

Yaakov felt his heart give a jump. Could the rabbi know what was going on?

"We have to find out if there is a possibility of a *get*," he said.

Yaakov gave a long sigh of relief, which was almost a groan.

"Also, we have to find him. Have you any idea where he could be?"

"Not at all," said Yaakov. "He caught the Cape Town-Johannesburg plane, midnight flight, *Motzei Shabbos*."

"Did you see him board the plane?" asked the rabbi.

"No, actually not. I didn't wait. He hadn't even gone through yet. He was about forty minutes early."

"Could he have gone somewhere else?" asked the rabbi.

Yaakov frowned.

"His father thought there was a chance he might have gone to Durban, to his old home," said Rabbi Weinstein. "Perhaps we could check that with the airport."

Rabbi and student went to the office and they phoned the airport, only to find that they could not obtain a list of names of people on that flight.

"All I can tell you is that that plane was rescheduled for two hours later," the airline employee said, about to put the phone down.

"No, wait," said Yaakov. "Wasn't there another midnight

flight? Isn't there a plane to Durban?"

"Yes, a special flight for the December holidays," said the man. "That left on time."

They phoned back to Ari's father and gave him the information.

"Have you any idea how we could find him on the South Coast?" the rabbi asked.

"I can probably make a few calls, but I have to wait till morning," said Mr. Isaacson. "But Rabbi, please explain more of this *get* thing to me. Surely there must be something we can do about it? You mentioned a kosher marriage. Does that mean an Orthodox marriage?"

"It isn't as simple as that," the rabbi said. "A marriage must be performed in the presence of kosher *eidim*, witnesses. Therefore, some civil or Reform marriages could be disqualified in Jewish law. But we have to know the exact details, all the details."

Again the father broke down.

"Please help us, Rabbi. I cannot bear to see my son so hurt. He's my oldest son, Rabbi. I was becoming so proud of him. He is a very, very special boy."

"I know," said the rabbi.

"I will do anything, absolutely anything that I can to help him."

"We'll be in contact in the morning," said the rabbi.

"Please call me as soon as you have some news."

Rabbi Weinstein turned to Yaakov. "You can handle my car, can't you?" he asked. "If we trace him to Durban, perhaps you could go and fetch him. In the meanwhile, I want you to get some sleep tonight. When did you last sleep properly, Yaakov?"

He thought for a few seconds. "Almost a week ago," he said.

This time, however, having shared the burden with someone more than adequate to deal with it, Yaakov found he could sleep.

He was awakened by Rabbi Weinstein coming into his room.

"I want you to drive down straight after you have *davened.* My wife has been preparing food for you. Mr. Isaacson has phoned me. He made several calls in Durban and the South Coast and eventually phoned a Mrs. McNeally, caretaker of the building Ari and his mother used to live in. Fortunately, the caretaker is still there.

"Ari went to see her on Sunday. They had a long chat. Apparently he told her he was broken-hearted over a girl. She even knew the name, Brocha. She knows he has a room somewhere, but she is not sure exactly where. She gave Mr. Isaacson the name of the agencies down there and we have the addresses for you."

He handed it to Yaakov.

"I want you to tell Ari I know about the problem. We are with him, completely with him. Tell him not to worry. The situation must be investigated. Things need not be as hopeless as they seem. We want him back immediately."

Twenty-Six

Rabbi Weinstein was unable to sleep. He sat in his study, a *Gemara* in front of him. A cold, anxious feeling alternated with waves of fear inside him.

What had he done? What kind of *shidduch* had he made? And yet it had felt so right, so good. Every instinct within him told him that it was a very special *shidduch* and that Ari was, of course, a kosher Jew. But it seemed his instincts could have been wrong. It was, *chas veshalom*, extremely likely that Ari wasn't.

He should have investigated Ari's background more closely. But the boy himself had not known. It had come out purely by accident. It might have never come out at all, or come out when Ari and Brocha were married and had children.

He shuddered at the thought. Those children, too, would not be kosher Jews, and that too would be irreversible.

If he had found out that Ari had not been Jewish, that would have been a tragedy itself but at least he could have, and would have, undergone conversion to become Jewish. There was no remedy for this one. There was nothing to be done if it was established finally and completely that Ari had been born *halachically* blemished.

He knew this problem was increasing in the Jewish world, and that great *halachic* minds were working on it. He remembered a case in point, a *baalas teshuvah* on the other side of town, who, when it had been finally established that she was kosher, had fainted from relief and shock.

He thought about Rabbi Goldstein, his best friend since *yeshivah* days. What had he done to him? What had he led him into? A wave of guilt and terror overcame him. He should phone him straightaway. What would he say to Rabbi Goldstein?

But something inside of him seemed to cry out against doing that. What if Ari were found to be a kosher Jew, or what if some *heter* was found? But Rabbi Goldstein was a person who insisted on everything, not only his meat, being completely *glatt*, with no question. Would he be happy with a *heter*?

But what if there was a *get*? Could there be a *get*? They hadn't even investigated that, and with that he decided to give the matter a week. After all, the wedding wasn't until *Nissan*. This was *Kislev*. Another week might make all the difference in the world here, and mean very little in England.

He thought about Ari, his student, and as he did so, tears began to stream down his cheeks. He was a student they had all come to love. He was quite sure that Ari was a kosher Jew. But was that enough?

When Ari was learning or *davening* it would seem that he radiated a certain *kedushah*, so that even he, the *rosh yeshivah*, was awed by it.

He had a sincerity and a commitment which stood out.

And of course, there was his brilliant way of analyzing a *Gemara*. It surely must be that Ari was a kosher Jew.

Where was Ari? Was he safe? Would he come back?

His head was beginning to ache. This was more painful than anything he had experienced as a *rosh yeshivah*. It was as if he had been given a glimpse of Gehinnom.

Rabbi Weinstein was not the only one unable to sleep that night. Even after the second phone call from him, Mr. Isaacson sat next to the phone, staring into space. The house was deathly quiet, which could be expected at that late hour, or rather, this extremely early hour. He, too, had developed a roaring headache and a feeling as if his stomach and intestines had been twisted into several knots.

What had they done to their son? They hadn't meant to do anything bad to him. It was true they had not been *frum*. But they had him circumcised and even *bar-mitzvahed*. They hadn't really kept any of the Jewish laws, but it seemed that neither did their neighbors and friends. After all, didn't everyone do what they wanted, with the idea that one day they might keep kosher or even a bit of *Shabbos*, feeling they could come back and start doing things whenever, if ever, they were ready?

There was always a way back. But in this, apparently there wasn't. He had never in his wildest dreams thought that there could be this kind of seriousness of consequence to disregarding Jewish law. Could they have spoiled it for their son? He had been so happy for his son.

His intestines seemed to give another twist, and he doubled over in pain. This was getting to him, really getting to him.

Why did he have such overwhelming feelings of guilt? Well, it wasn't he who had refused a *get* or had neglected one, but on the other hand, when he had divorced his wife, he hadn't even offered her one.

He should be more careful.

Another thing which worried him was the question of Jules and Debby. He remembered vaguely that he had said something to Ari about it, but he could not remember the answer he had gotten from him. If he hadn't gotten a *get* and he had married again, would there be something wrong with Jules' and Debby's birth? Sheila had never been married, so it didn't concern her, but he was, then, as it were, married to two women. He would have to speak to Rabbi Weinstein about it first thing the next day.

He kept seeing his oldest son's face in front of him. First, he saw him the way he had fetched him from the airport, so completely happy and excited. And then he would saw him the way he left, looking ill and shocked and full of despair. Well, the situation did look desperate. Why hadn't he known that one could take such an irreversible step? Why hadn't he been taught more by his own parents?

But, he had resisted it when Anthony had wanted to become more *frum*.

Sheila and he had hurt Ari in so many ways. They had mocked and criticized him and tried to cut off his relationship with the Levys. But he had persisted until he was now almost a rabbi, engaged to a *rosh yeshivah's* daughter.

But was he still engaged? He could no longer marry her. What was he going to do with his life? Why had they not known? And then he thought of Jules. He knew that they were being hard on him as well.

They had been so angry when Jules had started cooking for himself, and he had shown himself to be quite a good cook. Shouldn't it have broken their hearts when they saw him making *kiddush* for himself, eating a solitary *Shabbos* meal and carefully lighting the *Chanukah* candles by himself? He had not been allowed to go to the Levy's home, though Mr. Isaacson suspected there had been some contact.

But perhaps they could have allowed a little more, or taken some interest in his efforts to get the family to join him.

He remembered the time Jules had cooked a *Shabbos* meal for four and set four places on his desk. It had looked so beautiful and despite his pleas, they had refused to join him. Mr. Isaacson felt sick as he thought about it. He wanted his children and his family to be Jewish, of course he did. Perhaps he should allow Jules more. After all, from what he heard at the office, there were parents who were having to deal with drug problems with their children. Was it so bad that Jules wanted to be religious?

Was Zevi such a bad friend for him? He certainly would not lead him into drugs or take him to discos.

To his surprise, even Sheila had mentioned that a few days ago. They would have to reconsider their attitude to their children's religion. In fact, perhaps they had to reconsider their attitude to their own.

But now he had to think about Anthony.

As soon as he could, he would try to trace him in Durban or the South Coast. He hoped with all his heart that he was there, because, if not, where could he be?

He tried and tried to think, but his mind kept going blank. He was tired and he must sleep. However, as he discovered through the night, sleep would not come.

Twenty-Seven

Ari turned and turned in his bed. He was thirsty, very thirsty. His head ached and he felt hot, cold and shivery all at the same time. What was the time? He felt as if he had been asleep for hours, but he had been conscious of periods of wakefulness, where he had drunk all the water he could to quench his overpowering thirst. He remembered trying to learn and falling asleep over the *Gemara*, hardly having any strength to lift his head.

Strength? He had no energy at all. Why did his whole body feel so heavy?

His watch said nine o'clock. What day was it? He knew the day, it was Monday. Yesterday, Sunday, he had visited his old apartment. He tried to get up, and almost immediately got back into bed. He was weak, very weak. He must be ill. He shut his eyes again.

He was awakened by a knocking at the door. He stumbled out of bed to open the door, almost fainting from the exertion. He gave a gasp as he saw Yaakov, and Yaakov looked shocked when he saw him.

"Ari, you are ill!" he said. "Your face is all red and your eyes have dark rings under them."

"I didn't sleep well last night," said Ari. "I was very restless, and hot and shivery. I think maybe I have the flu."

"It looks that way," said Yaakov. "I am going to call a doctor for you."

"No, don't worry," said Ari. "It's probably one of those twenty-four hour things. But Yaakov," Ari seemed suddenly to realize something, "Yaakov, what are you doing here? I mean, this is Durban. How did you find me? You are supposed to be in Cape Town."

"I arrived at the *yeshivah* yesterday," said Yaakov, "and you weren't there. I was very, very worried."

"But Yaakov, why did you go back early? You were only due on Tuesday."

"I did arrive on Tuesday," said Yaakov, looking puzzled. "I left this morning."

"What day is it?" asked Ari, sitting bolt upright.

"It is Wednesday," said Yaakov.

Ari gave a groan. "But what happened to Monday and Tuesday? I went to bed last night and it was Sunday. Maybe I really have been ill."

"You most definitely look as though you have," said Yaakov. "I am going to call the doctor. Do you know where there is one?"

"At the shopping center, a kilometer up the main Coastal road," said Ari. "At least, there was a group of doctors there when we were here last," he added.

Yaakov lost no time in calling him. The doctor on call would be there within the hour. He went back to Ari's room.

"Yaakov, how did you find me?" asked Ari.

"Your dad helped us figure out that you were here," said

Yaakov. "He was extremely worried about you. So was Rabbi Weinstein."

Ari suddenly withdrew.

"You told him about me?" he asked, almost accusingly.

"No, I didn't," said Yaakov. "But he became very worried because he saw I was very worried, and he phoned my father and then your father. Your father told him everything."

"Did my father understand the problem?" asked Ari, wearily. Oh, why were waves and waves of dizziness coming over him?

"Rabbi Weinstein explained it to him, and he understood eventually. He wants to do everything he can. He has been extremely worried. He didn't sleep at all last night."

"Dad?" asked Ari. "He was that worried?"

"Oh yes," said Yaakov.

"Yaakov," said Ari, "I want you to know how I appreciate this. I might not be a kosher Jew, and you came all this way to find me."

"You are my friend, my best friend!" said Yaakov. "Also, Rabbi Weinstein sent me. I came in his car, you know." He waved his hand towards the door. "We are going back in it."

"I can't go back there. What does Rabbi Weinstein think?"

"He told me to tell you not to worry."

"How can I not worry?" asked Ari.

"There are some *heterim* that can be investigated. I mean, the wedding of your mother and Donald Levine might not have been kosher. There might not have been kosher witnesses."

"I am sure there weren't," said Ari, a ray of light seeming to break through the darkness that had engulfed them for so long. "Does that mean that there is hope for me?"

"It seems so," said Yaakov. "But Rabbi Weinstein wants

you to investigate all that and see what you can unearth."

Ari closed his eyes, and Yaakov was again struck by how ill he looked. Everything was silent, and Yaakov realized that Ari had fallen asleep.

Yaakov sat at his friend's bedside, studying *Gemara,* until there was a knock at the door.

A young doctor was standing outside. He looked amazed to see Yaakov.

"You called me," he began. "I am Dr. Segal."

Yaakov moved away and the doctor saw Ari.

"Doesn't look too well," he said. "How long has he been ill? Why didn't you call me before?"

Yaakov explained that he had only arrived on the South Coast a couple of hours ago.

The doctor went over to Ari, who had opened his eyes. The doctor examined him thoroughly.

"Hmm," he said, "not quite as bad as I thought. You have a virus that is going around. Usually takes three to four days to work itself out. You seem to be at the end of it. But you seem to have been quite ill," he said.

He looked at Ari carefully.

"Is there anything worrying you?" he asked.

"Yes," said Ari, "I was supposed to get married. Now I think it might be off."

Yaakov started at his quick reply. A good one it certainly was. The doctor understood immediately.

"Don't take it so hard, young man," he said. "There are many pebbles on the beach. But I know it is difficult. At the time it is happening, it seems one will never recover. But then one does. It is as if the sun suddenly comes through the clouds and we are surprised, because we had come to feel that it had disappeared forever. We have forgotten even what it was like to experience any kind of happiness."

Ari nodded.

"Good food, plenty of rest and . . ."

"Can I go back to Johannesburg today with Yaakov?" asked Ari.

"Absolutely not," said the doctor, frowning. "I want this young man to care for you today, and I will see you tomorrow morning. I start my rounds around seven o'clock. If I am satisfied that you can travel, you may travel. Otherwise, you will wait another day. You will get there before *Shabbos*," he added.

He looked at Yaakov.

"I presume you can organize kosher food for an extra day."

"I have brought some with me," said Yaakov. "Probably enough for several days."

"May Ari get up at all to get to a telephone?" he asked. "We need to make some calls."

"I think so," said the doctor. "Give him something to eat, let him rest a bit and then take him." He went over to Ari and spoke to him.

"Ari," he said, "when a person is unhappy, the way you are, they lose the will to fight off an illness. I want you to concentrate on getting better. Eat something. You've got your whole life ahead of you, young man. Don't fret it away. You *frum* guys have a wealth of inspiration you can hold on to. I used to envy the *frum* guys in medical school. They had an inner strength that the others didn't have. Hold on to that, Ari. When a person is ill or depressed it seems it might have gone. But you guys have it, I can see that. I want to see it glowing out of you tomorrow morning."

He left, leaving both Ari and Yaakov somewhat stunned.

Yaakov set about making sure that Ari would eat. He was horrified that he had only eaten *matzoh* and drunk water.

"It wasn't that," said Ari. "I was ill."

"You certainly were, in more ways than one," said Yaakov. "Thank goodness I found you."

"*Baruch Hashem,*" said Ari.

Mr. Isaacson was extremely relieved to hear his son on the phone.

"Listen, Anthony," he said, "I want you to come down here as soon as possible, as soon as you are well. We are going to speak to people together. We will find out as much as we can, and if there was a *get,* we will find it. We first have to see if the wedding was kosher. I am taking a few days leave to go with you."

He spoke for a fairly long time, and then handed the phone to Jules.

"Ari," he said excitedly. "Ari, are you all right? Dad has been speaking to Rabbi Levy, and I am going there for *Shabbos*. Can you believe it? The whole of *Shabbos*."

Their next phone call was to Rabbi Weinstein. He reassured Ari that the position was far from hopeless, and it just had to be investigated. When he put down the phone, Yaakov saw something of the old Ari returning.

"Let's learn," he said. "We have so much to catch up, and we have only until tomorrow morning to do so."

Perhaps the doctor would have felt that this was a strange way to look after a patient, but Yaakov felt there was a strong possibility that he would thoroughly approve.

Twenty-Eight

Rabbi Weinstein was shocked at the change in Ari. Where was the confident, brilliant student he had known over the past few years? True, Ari had always been a little hesitant and reticent, but he had never seen him like this. He almost seemed to want to shrink into the walls. Apart from this, and more obviously, he looked as if he had been extremely ill. True, he had had a rather bad dose of influenza, but to look like this one would surely have had to have been ill for weeks or even months. Ari had been well and happy only a week ago.

He invited the boy to sit down, and tried not to flinch as he looked into the eyes of one who obviously had passed through severe emotional, and even physical, pain. He himself was feeling quite sick from the whole situation.

"You have been through a bad time, Ari," he began.

Ari nodded.

"I want you to know that we are completely with you. I want you to know that whatever happens, you are a student of this *yeshivah* and will always be one. In fact, after I am through with you, I want you to go into the study hall and continue with your learning."

Ari smiled. These words meant a lot to him. It seemed to be years and years ago, a lifetime ago, that he had been learning in the study hall.

"I also want to tell you something else," said the rabbi, "and I know Yaakov gave you part of this message. I want to tell you not to worry. The position is far from hopeless, and it has to be gone into completely. You are not the first person, and unfortunately not the last person, to go through this. We need information, a great deal of information, and after *Shabbos* I want you to take the midnight plane back to Cape Town. Yaakov will see that you actually get onto it," he said, smiling.

"You will spend next week and the week after and maybe even the week after that, using your time to make these investigations. Your father is taking leave from work so that he can help you.

"It could be that there were no kosher *eidim* at the original wedding. This is often so with Reform or with court weddings. Even that, of course, isn't simple. It has to be gone into thoroughly. If we find that it was a completely kosher wedding, there are other things which need to be investigated. Don't worry, we must just work hard at it."

The rabbi stopped, hoping that Ari would not notice his own desperate, almost overwhelming anxiety.

Ari had hardly spoken during this time. But he suddenly looked straight at the rabbi.

"About Brocha," he began. "What about the *shidduch*? They will have to be told. Have you told them?"

"I have thought and thought about it, and I decided that we should wait until you have done these investigations. Then, if is necessary, I will speak to Rabbi Goldstein."

Ari gave a sigh. "Do you think there is any hope?' he asked.

"Yes, yes I do," said the rabbi. "We must just search and find. Hashem hasn't brought you this far just to desert you," he added.

"I know," said Ari. "But, Rabbi Weinstein, please tell me if this is true: if my mother never got a *get* and there was a kosher wedding to her first husband, and none of the *heterim* apply, can I still learn? Can I still do the *semichah* program? Can I still serve Hashem?"

"Definitely," said the rabbi. "There is a lot written about that. But Ari, I believe deep inside that we are going to find out that you are all right."

Even as he said this, he felt a tinge of doubt. He hoped and prayed with all his heart that it would, in fact, be good.

"What about Rabbi Levy?" asked Ari. "Does he know about it all?

"He knows something is very wrong," said the *rosh yeshivah*. "I think your father might be going to speak to him. I am actually not sure."

"Maybe he should know," said Ari.

The rabbi thought for a few moments.

"Yes, I think he should be informed. There is no way he would let anyone else know about it, not even his family. Both you and your father need a great deal of support which he can give you, and I am very far from Cape Town. Also, Rabbi Levy might be aware that certain things are important that your father and even you might miss. I think it would be good for you to speak to him. He has been your *rav* since you were a child, and he has taken you through a great many things."

"I would like to phone him," said Ari. "I would like to speak to him, but I don't want to be the one to tell him. I won't know how to tell him."

Rabbi Weinstein looked at his watch.

"Give me an hour," he said, "and then check with me and call him after that. And Ari, don't worry. I want you to eat properly and to sleep properly and start to get into the learning. Next week will be very busy for you."

It seemed strange being in the study hall once more, and he was glad that Yaakov was already there, learning, waiting for him to come and learn with him.

For a few minutes, Ari had a tremendous sense of non-belonging, as if he was rejected by all. But he was not prepared for the reception he did get. Rejection would have been preferable.

"Ari! Here comes the *chassan*," said Shmuel, coming over to welcome him. "Hey, you look sick. Aren't you well?"

"Flu," said Ari. Why hadn't he realized that the whole world didn't know of his problem?

Yerachmiel joined them.

"I see you are starving yourself. Nervous about the wedding?"

Ari blushed. What was he to say? They were hurting him so much, and yet there was no way they could know it.

Rabbi Feinstein came over to him and shook his hand. He had been away for several weeks, and had only heard about Ari's engagement when he got back.

"*Mazel tov*, Ari," he said warmly. "I was really happy to hear about you. I wasn't surprised, though, that you found such a good *shidduch*. I always had the highest opinion of you."

Ari felt he was going to faint. He sat down in the chair nearest to him.

"Sorry," he said. "I have just had the most rotten flu. I couldn't move for days." He looked up at the rabbi. "Thank you," he said. "I appreciate your words."

The other *bachurim* looked at him in concern.

"Hey," said Yerachmiel, "you really look ill. You look as if you have lost at least five kilos. Maybe you should still be in bed."

Yaakov had noticed what was going on and had joined them.

"Don't send away my *chavrusa*," he said. "I've missed him over the last few days. I will look after him very carefully and see to it that he doesn't work too hard."

He led Ari away from the young men around him. "I will put him to bed directly after we have finished," he said.

It took Ari some time to be able to get into the learning, but as soon as he did so, he found himself relaxing, as if he was turning to an eternal source of strength. He was beginning to understand on a different level how much of a refuge the sweetness of Torah could be. Not that in the past he had ever taken it for granted, but now it was to him like a cool, clear spring in a desert. He drank thirstily.

He returned to the dorm much later, really tired and not feeling all that well.

As he passed the notice board, someone called to him and handed him a letter from Brocha. He held on to it, not wanting to open it. After all, it didn't refer to him any more.

Alone in his room, he stared at it for some minutes and then put it into his overnight bag. He would take it with him to Cape Town.

There was no way he could read it now. There was no way he could respond to it. He would read it later, much later.

Twenty-Nine

It was a different Mr. Isaacson who met his son at the airport on that Sunday night. Ari noticed this immediately. It was as if his father had suddenly become more human, more vulnerable, more friendly and accepting.

He helped Ari carry his bags to the car, saying that they had a lot to do together and that he hoped Ari was feeling better.

As they drove through the night streets, Ari immediately realized that his father's attitude to *Yiddishkeit* had changed. He was talking, now, about eventually keeping kosher at least at home and about the enjoyable *Shabbos* Jules had spent with the Levys.

In spite of his own turmoil, Ari was very excited about this.

"Anthony," said his father, a few minutes away from his home, "Anthony, I want to tell you that I am sorry for all kinds of things. Sheila and I have been talking, and we realize that we gave you a very difficult time about your commitment to Judaism.

"Now we see that our distance from Judaism nearly caused a tragedy for you. I hope we can rectify it. We must do something to change it. But Anthony, I didn't know the laws about a *get*. I had, of course, heard of a Jewish divorce, but I thought it was just some traditional religious thing of no real importance. I thought the civil divorce was important, and there is no way I would have married your mother without that."

They arrived at the house and Mr. Isaacson led Ari inside.

"We will have plenty of time to talk in the days ahead. I have taken leave from work to help you resolve the situation, full time.

"And Anthony," he said, "perhaps you can teach me a little bit also. Just enough, maybe, to follow in *shul*."

The next morning, Ari awoke at the sound of a gentle knock on his door. Yehudah came in. He was fully dressed.

"We have to be in *shul* soon. Get dressed, Ari," he said, and then he gave a whoop of delight. "You see, Ari, now that you are going to be a rabbi and marry a famous rabbi's daughter, Dad's letting me come to *shul* with you. I've never been able to go on a weekday morning before. We are going to have breakfast with the Levys after *davening*."

They were soon walking along the familiar roads towards the Levy's home and *shul*. Yehudah was telling him excitedly about his *Shabbos* with the Levys.

"After I tell you this, please tell me about Brocha," said Yehudah. "I know you like to talk about her all the time," he said, thinking of his previous visit.

Ari said nothing. Yehudah continued to tell him about *Shabbos*.

"There were all kinds of people at the *Shabbos* table," he said. "Most of them weren't even *frum* at all. They kept talking about the strange ways of Orthodox Jews. Oh, and there was also Zevi's latest pupil, a boy in his school. He is *frum*, of course."

"His *chavrusa*, you mean?" asked Ari.

"No, not really," said Yehudah. "Zevi is teaching him Hebrew. They started from *alef-beis*. But he has been *frum* all his life."

Ari nodded, waiting for an explanation from his younger brother.

"He has always been in a *yeshivah*, but he had . . . what is it called? He had difficulty reading."

"Dyslexia?" said Ari.

"That's it," said Yehudah. "He was eventually able to read English, but his Hebrew dragged and dragged behind. Although he is a very clever boy and is very good in some subjects, he could hardly read a *pasuk*. But he remembered his doctor saying that around the time of his *bar-mitzvah*, the dyslexia would begin to improve, and if he really wanted to he could start learning to read Hebrew then, right from the beginning.

"He knew Zevi would be a good teacher and that he wouldn't laugh at him learning pre-grade stuff and all that. And he has come a long, long way, almost up to his class. He reads well now, but still a bit slowly. He told us all about it at the *Shabbos* table."

Ari was thoughtful. It must have taken a great deal of courage for the boy to go back to the beginning. Without this, he might have floundered with Hebrew forever.

They arrived at *shul*, Ari realizing with surprise that for a few minutes he had forgotten about his own problem, being absorbed in the details of Zevi's new pupil.

However, as he entered the *shul*, the sick, anxious, heavy feeling came back to him. The last *Shabbos* he had been here, he had felt that life for him had completely ended.

He had not phoned Rabbi Levy from Johannesburg. Rabbi Weinstein had not been able to speak to him until quite late, and Ari had felt that as he was going down to Cape Town immediately after *Shabbos*, it would be better to speak to him face to face. He wondered how he had reacted to the news.

However, as the rabbi saw him enter the *shul* with Yehudah, he gave him a look which seemed to say that he understood everything.

The rabbi made arrangements to see him in the *shul* office immediately afterwards, while Zevi and Yehudah spent some time learning.

Ari appreciated the fact that they would not speak in the rabbi's home. He knew that with Rabbi Levy, he would not be able to hold back the tears, and he did not want any of the Levys or in fact his brother, to see him so vulnerable.

He was not wrong. As soon as he was closed in with the rabbi in his office, he found himself crying and crying, feeling he would never stop.

He knew that Rabbi Weinstein had reassured him to some extent, but he also knew that he might find nothing to improve his position. He himself did not count on some *heter*. He felt that he could not marry Brocha if there was the slightest doubt as to his being a kosher Jew. Amidst sobs, he told this to the rabbi, who said that Rabbi Weinstein had explained the position very fully.

"Ari," he said, when the tears had abated somewhat, "Ari, I don't want to talk about what is or isn't going to happen to you, or whether you are or are not a kosher Jew, as you put it. I hope and pray, and I really believe, that things will go well for you. But Ari, whatever you are, you are a Jew. You are Hashem's child. You were given your particular set of circumstances by Hashem. It isn't your fault. And in whatever position a person is placed, whether rich or poor, Kohein,

Levi, Yisrael, or as you put it, kosher or not kosher, that is where you find yourself. From there, you must serve Hashem completely.

"Even though there are major problems with a non-kosher Jew as regards to marriage, he can still study Torah and become great in the study of Torah. He can still *daven* with all his heart. He could, in fact, be a strong inspiration to others.

"One's faith and trust, Ari," he said, "have to go beyond all that. Whatever happens, you will marry the person you are supposed to marry, the other half of your *neshamah*, or if necessary, you won't marry at all. Our attachment and our service of Hashem is higher than that, deeper than that. If you strengthen that, Ari, you will get through whatever you have to get through."

He looked at the tear-stained, white face of the young man sitting in front of him, and Ari felt as if the rabbi's eyes pierced to his very soul.

"Ari, believe me, I understand how much all this is hurting you. I know how much it is tearing you apart and breaking your heart. I know that, Ari. But know, even in the center of all this, Ari, you can drink from the waters of Torah and you can become close to Hashem in a way that you perhaps couldn't do before. In these kinds of times, you can experience what life is all about through learning and *davening*."

For a few seconds the rabbi saw a glimpse of the Ari he knew. He even smiled a little as he spoke.

"Rabbi Levy, I am seeing some of that already. With all this happening to me, I could experience something in the *davening* and learning which I hadn't felt before. It was as if I was very, very thirsty and when I started learning *Gemara*, I found that that thirst was being quenched. I hadn't noticed it so much before, because I hadn't been so thirsty."

They spoke for a long time until Ari felt ready to go with his father on their investigations, as if his whole life and faith no longer hung on the outcome.

Thirty

Mr. Isaacson crept quietly, almost stealthily into Ari's room, an old photograph album under his arm.

"I really don't want anyone else to see this. Sheila might be hurt knowing I still have it. But I think these pictures might be of some use to us."

He sat on the bed and asked Ari to sit next to him as he opened the album to the first page.

Ari gave a gasp, and he felt tears coming into his eyes. Oh, why did he cry so easily these days!

There was his mother. Never in his life had he seen her look so serene. She was sitting on a large rock, the ocean to one side of her and the Muisenberg Mountains on the other. Her long, honey-colored hair was blowing in the wind, and she was smiling–no, she was laughing. Everything about her radiated happiness and a love of life.

He could not stop looking at her.

He turned the page and turned another. Here again were photos of his mother, some of them with his father, and it was obvious that they were very happy together. They appeared to have been mountain climbers. Several of the photos showed them in semi-mountain gear, and they appeared to have been doing a fairly difficult climb.

"I have never seen these pictures before," Ari said. "I have seen pictures of Mum at school, but then all the rest seem to be missing until after the divorce."

He paged on. How could two people who had been so obviously happy together have come to hate one another so much?

He paused to look at an enlarged photograph of his mother and father taken on a walk up Chapman's Peak. The route was dotted with wildflowers. On the side of the mountain was Hout Bay and on the other side of the mountain was a glimpse of another part of the ocean in the far, far distance. Could it have been Fish Hoek?

"That was when we decided to get engaged," his father said. "It was as if the whole world was ahead of us."

Then came the wedding pictures. Ari was disappointed, in a way, that his mother had not worn a traditional bridal gown for the ceremony.

There was only one picture taken outside the court, in which the bride wore a stylish pale blue outfit. For the reception, bride and groom had worn something more formal, and her dress did, in fact, mimic the traditional bridal dress. It was long, lacy and white except for tiny blue beads and a blue rose pinned in her hair. Mr. Isaacson wore a traditional dress-suit.

Ari was especially interested in pictures of the wedding guests. They discussed several, but it seemed that probably none would have been able to help them. Of his mother's family, only her brother and an uncle had been at the wedding. Both of them were dead now, the brother having been killed in a car crash.

The other guests were mutual friends, mostly from their places of work.

His mother had been working in an insurance company, and his father had been working in a civil engineering consultants' firm. He pointed out several people they had been friendly with. There was not even a flicker of someone being *frum*. Most of the guests had not been Jewish. If only his mother's first wedding was like this!

They paged through, until the pictures showed his mother pregnant and then with him as a baby.

He had seen pictures of himself as a baby and as a toddler, but all those photos had been of himself and his mother. Now he saw himself being carried and diapered and bathed and loved by a very proud father. Again he felt the tears starting to well up. The rest of the book was devoted to him and the way he was progressing. There were pictures of him crawling, taking his first few steps, riding a tricycle. In one photograph, he sat on a big rocking horse, his father standing next to him. Father and son wore identical jerseys.

"Your mother knitted those for us," his father said, laughing. "She said that we were beginning to look so alike that she wanted us to dress alike. She didn't carry it too far, thank goodness."

"Were you happy with Mum?" he said, wonderingly.

"Oh, yes," he said.

"What happened, then?" he asked. "Was it because you met Aunt Sheila?"

"No, no, of course not," his father said. "I met Sheila long after we were divorced. Court divorce, that is," he said, blushing.

Suddenly a shadow crossed his face.

"I am sorry, son," he said. "I know I have said this before, but I cannot say it often enough. I am so, so sorry. You see, I thought I made the mistake again. I had two more children without giving your mother a *get*."

"That's different," said Ari. "It isn't good, but there is no problem with the children. It is only where the woman needs a *get* and doesn't have one."

"I know that now," said his father, "but it gave me a lot of soul searching and heartache. I thought I had ruined three of my children's lives, instead of only one."

Tears started to fall from his eyes.

"Oh, Anthony, my Anthony, I didn't know, I really didn't know."

Ari put his arm around his father's shoulder. "I know you didn't, Dad, I know you didn't. And don't worry about Jules and Debby. They are all right."

"I know," said his father. "I checked it with Rabbi Weinstein, and then I asked Rabbi Levy again, just to make sure."

"You know, Anthony, South African Jews are strange. Our parents and grandparents were very religious in Lithuania. When they came to South Africa, some remained religious but most dropped their *Yiddishkeit* somewhere on the boat coming over. *Yiddishkeit* was part of the old country and had nothing to do with the modern world. Those people who did bring their *Yiddishkeit* here were regarded as being part of the old country and of the old world. They somehow could not put it across to the next generation. And yet, there always remained something. Jews held onto some of the things that their parents held dear. They never quite lost touch.

"The rabbi was still quite important to many families. But I think that very, very few people know that by not getting a *get*, you can have children who can no longer marry a proper Jew. People know that even if they convert, they can still come back. I didn't know, Ari. I don't think people know they can do something so terrible to their children, so terrible that it can't be reversed. Ari, we have got to let them know about it!"

Mr. Isaacson looked dejectedly at the photograph album.

"There doesn't seem to be anything helpful here," he said. "I thought it might make me remember something." He began to close the book.

"No, go on Dad," said Ari. "I want to see those pictures. There are only a few more pages."

He saw himself again with his father. He didn't remember any of these things, though of course he was only a toddler. He saw a photo of himself with his father looking into the lion habitat at the zoo. He saw himself riding on a pony being led by a young man, his father following uncertainly behind. There was a picture of his father hugging him tight.

"Dad," said Ari, "you really loved me, didn't you?"

"I adored you," his father said.

"But afterwards . . ." began Ari.

"When you were taken from me," said Mr. Isaacson, "it was as if someone had come and wrenched out my heart. I would dream of you calling me in the night, asking for water, asking me to change you. And then I would wake up and you weren't there. I thought I would never recover. My treasure, my pride, my lovely, beautiful, precious son had been taken away to Natal."

"I didn't know, Dad," said Ari. "I didn't realize that."

Mr. Isaacson shut the book with a loud click. "That's past," he said. "Now you are my son and you are here, and we have a lot to do. There is nothing in these photos, nothing to jog or stir my memory. I haven't opened this album for years and years. It was always too painful, but I thought it would have something we could work on. We will have to try something else."

"Dad, before you put it away, please show me those pictures of Mum again. She looked so gracious, so happy, and so did you."

They once more looked through the first few pages.

"If only she could talk to us and tell us, we would know," said Ari.

"I don't know," said his father, "I can't think of anything.

"In all these photos, it is just you two," said Ari. "There was no one else, no one else." He stared at the enlarged one of his parents on Chapman's Peak and then said suddenly, "Hey, wait a minute, Dad. You couldn't have been alone, the two of you. I mean, who took the photo?"

A look of excitement appeared on Mr. Isaacson's face.

"Of course! How could I have forgotten! We were with Sam Feinberg, Sam and his sister Susan. They often went climbing with us. They had been friends of Sylvia, your mother, for many years. I think they had all been in school together. They weren't at our wedding because he was transferred to South West Africa for some years, and Susan went on to Johannesburg some time before. I haven't seen them since, but when I first met them, we went everywhere with them. They must have been at your mother's first wedding to Donald Levine!"

"But, Dad, how will we find them?" asked Ari, not wanting to dampen his father's enthusiasm. "Susan is sure to be married now, so she won't be Mrs. Feinberg, and Sam is in South West Africa.

"No, he was coming back, he was definitely coming back. His company moved him all over. He was in shipping."

"Do you remember the name of his company?" asked Ari. "Although he surely won't be with them now."

"He could be," said his father. "People don't always move companies. If not with them he could be with another company like that. The only trouble is that then he could be in any of the coastal towns, even Port Elizabeth or Durban.

"Ari, as soon as the businesses open tomorrow, we will phone the shipping companies and find out where he is. Even if he is overseas, Ari, we will find him. He is the only person whom we might be able to speak to. I have thought and thought over the last few days. There just is no one else. In fact, I would not have thought of them if you hadn't asked me who took the photo. What a strange thing memory is!"

Thirty-One

It was already eleven o'clock on Monday morning. Nothing seemed to be coming up. No one had heard of Sam Feinberg. Surely they were not going to find this to be a dead end? Ari and his father seemed to be quite desperate.

"What can I do?" Mr. Isaacson asked some particularly obliging clerk that he was speaking to.

"Whom have you contacted already?" asked the man.

Mr. Isaacson gave him at least twenty-five names.

"That covers pretty much all of them. In fact, you have one or two even I didn't know about. Are you sure this Sam Feinberg, as you call him, was in shipping?"

"Yes," he said, "I am quite sure. He was definitely in shipping."

"He didn't go into any kind of overland transport and trading company, did he?" he asked. "I mean, that would deal with people up north. It is quite a specialized thing, what with sanctions and everything."

David Isaccson was ready to clutch at any straw. He took

down six names, and struck oil on his second phone call.

"Sam Feinberg?" the man said. "Yes, of course he is with us. Has been with us for the last eight years. I will give you his number. He is not actually in Cape Town at the moment, but is in Kopville, about a hundred kilometers from here. We have offices down there."

He gave him the number, and Mr. Isaacson put down the phone and stared at it for a few minutes.

"Do you have his number?" asked Ari.

"Yes," said his father. "I feel quite nervous to contact him. I just hope he can help us."

Eventually, he plucked up courage and dialed the number, only to find that the man would be out of the office until three o'clock.

"We can't waste time," said his father. "We must go out there ourselves. If we leave soon, we should get there at three, and then we can talk to him face to face. This is going to be too difficult over the telephone."

He then redialed the number, this time speaking to Sam Feinberg's secretary.

No, three o'clock would not be convenient, as he was coming in for another appointment. However, seeing they were old friends, she would give him the message that they would be there to see him at four. He would finally be free at that time.

Four and a half hours to wait. That would be an eternity.

They phoned through to Rabbi Weinstein to tell him that they had traced someone whom, they were sure, had attended the first wedding. The rabbi was delighted. All they had to do was to check where it was held, and more or less who attended the wedding. Then they could investigate from there. He was sure it would have been in a Reform synagogue, or in court. There couldn't have been kosher witnesses!

Ari could scarcely concentrate on the miles and miles of countryside they went through. Neither could he find it within himself to speak too much. He was only vaguely aware of the mountains and valleys, historic towns and magnificent Cape-Dutch style homesteads they were passing. He kept having conversations with Sam Feinberg in his mind. In some of these, the man was declaring that he and his sister had been the only Jews at the wedding, besides the bride and groom. In another mind trip, he was telling him that the wedding had actually taken place on *Shabbos* somewhere on top of Table Mountain with a marriage officer who had been paid well for his excursion. To even attend that wedding, one would have had to be violate *Shabbos*.

But he knew these things were not going to be that easy. All he could hope for was a lead for the *Beis Din* to follow.

They arrived fifteen minutes early and sat in the waiting room, looking at the Finance and National Geographic magazines, scarcely concentrating. The minutes seemed to crawl by like hours.

Oh, why didn't Sam Feinberg hurry up with his interview? Didn't he realize that they could sit still no longer?

4:10 p.m., 4:20, 4:30. Still he did not come out. The secretary became apologetic.

"He knows you are here. It is just that he was a little late for his three o'clock appointment. He actually started it just before you came."

Both Ari and his father sighed and settled back to wait another half hour.

They were startled, however, by a buzzer, and were ushered into the man's office.

"David!" said the man, getting up from behind his desk. "I thought it had to be you when I heard the name. Are you in the business now?"

Was this in fact the slim, athletic Sam who he had known? He was now rotund and had lost most of his hair.

He shook Mr. Isaacson's hand warmly and then turned to Ari. "Is this your son?" he asked. Then he laughed. "How could I ask that question? He is the spitting image of you, except for the beard, of course.

"Hey, son, you look like a rabbi. Your great-grandmother would have been delighted to have a rabbi in the family."

Relieved that this man seemed to know his mother's family right back to her grandmother, Ari shook his hand. They all sat down.

"What brings you here?" asked Sam Feinberg. "Is it business or something else? I mean, it is good of you to look me up, but you must have a reason."

A look of concern crossed his face. "You are Sylvia's child, aren't you, Anthony? I can see that, though it takes a while to see the resemblance through your strong resemblance to your father. But I can see it in your expressions and way of speaking. I heard about your mother's death. I was devastated. So was my sister. We had been friends for so, so many years, since we were children, in fact."

Mr. Isaacson was about to tell him the reason for their visit when Sam Feinberg continued.

"I would never, ever have believed that her son would be religious, her son of all people." There were tears welling up in his eyes.

"Sorry," he said. "I want you to know that I am proud of you. I know that quite a few young people are taking to religion nowadays, and I feel it's a privilege for it to be someone I know, or, to be more correct, the son of someone I once knew." He paused, and again Ari's father tried to broach the subject of the wedding.

"You want to know about my sister, I am sure. She

married someone in Johannesburg, and they went to live in Pretoria. They have two children. He is not Jewish, of course. Afrikaans. But they are fairly happy. No one is *really* happy nowadays. But she must be fairly happy, because they have a lovely townhouse and each of them has a BMW. So they are happy and fulfilled and successful."

Even David Isaacson was struck by the emptiness of his logic, but he did not comment.

"Now," said Sam Feinberg, in a businesslike tone, "what can I do for you two gentlemen? Something in the business line?"

"No," said Mr. Isaacson. "This has nothing to do with business. Anthony is thinking of getting married, and we wanted to ask you a few questions."

"Go ahead," said Mr. Feinberg, changing to his semi-business tone.

"We wanted to know about Sylvia's first wedding, to Donald Levine. Did you attend it?"

"Oh yes, I did," he said, brightening.

He surely had good news for them.

"That was a very big wedding, a very fine wedding. I think there were three hundred people at the wedding, maybe even four hundred or even five hundred. They had planned a smaller one, but Sylvia's grandmother would not have it that way. This was her first grandchild, and it had to be special, and it was special."

"Was it an Orthodox wedding?" asked Ari, feeling his heart starting to beat fast.

"Oh, absolutely," said the man, smiling broadly. "Your great-grandmother was a very, very Orthodox woman. She wouldn't even drink tea in any of our houses. She was straight from Lithuania, and had left none of her customs behind. The rabbis seemed to get on with her. Great old lady she was in many ways, I suppose. But very strict and disapproving. There were plenty of rabbis at that wedding. It was one of the most Orthodox weddings I have ever attended."

Ari tried not to show that his world had once again collapsed around him. Mr. Isaacson was just staring straight in front of him.

Sam Feinberg was oblivious to their reaction. He kept reassuring them about the wedding, at each comment devastating them more and more.

"Old lady died shortly after," he said. "Then any Judaism that had been in that family collapsed. Not that anyone did anything, except when she was around. But while she was around, if she visited anyone's home, she would not eat there. They tried to convince her that they had some Jewish feeling by getting a *mezuzah* to put on the door and all that, and buying her some kosher biscuits.

"They dropped it very hard when she died. The pressure was completely off. But now look at it, it comes out in her great-grandson. Totally amazing, that is."

"Could you tell me some of the names of the rabbis who were there?" asked Ari.

"No, not at all," said the man. "I don't think I even asked them. But the rabbi who performed the service was Drotsky. He is mostly retired now, but I think he is still in Cape Town. He was working afterwards for some sort of Jewish organization."

He looked to see if his visitors had any questions, and with relief went on to talk about his own life. He had married. He had a double story house on six acres, not far away. He had done well, he felt. He had a swimming pool, a tennis court, he drove a Mercedes, his wife a BMW, and they had a child who was in metric. In fact, she had been getting quite good marks, and might even be in line for a distinction.

On the way back in the car, both Ari and his father were silent. The wedding was definitely absolutely kosher. There could be no doubt about that. They would just have to phone Rabbi Weinstein and let him know that their search was at an end.

David Isaacson found it difficult to concentrate on the road in front of him. His eyes kept misting over. How could life be so cruel, and to an innocent child who had only striven to do good!

Ari was almost numb from shock . . . Shock? He had expected it, hadn't he? He had known all the time that it wouldn't be good. He had to hold on to his faith, hold on to his faith and trust. Not that all would come right in that sense for him, but hold on to the fact that whatever his situation, Hashem had a purpose for him.

When Rabbi Weinstein heard the news, he was too shocked to speak. When the words finally came out, he felt as if they were travelling through him from a far, far distance. This seemed to be it! And yet, there was a glimmer of hope.

"Ari," he said to the boy whose voice sounded flat and dead, "Ari, we have to do more research. You have two things to do. Find out when your great-grandmother died. The marriage didn't last for long and if she was alive, she would have known to insist on a *get*.

"And Ari, go to Rabbi Drotsky. Have a chat with him. He will help you. I have heard of him, but Rabbi Levy will know where he is better than I do because he is in Cape Town.

"Ask him to do some research on this marriage. Maybe there was a *get*." With a fervent prayer, he put down the phone, noting that where he had been holding the receiver, it had become soaking wet.

Thirty-Two

It was not difficult to find Rabbi Drotsky. He had retired years ago, and spent his time helping the overworked rabbi of his old *shul* and ministering to a small Jewish Old Age Home, many of whose residents were in fact younger than he. True retirement was not for him. When anyone asked where and when he would finally retire, he always answered steadily, "In *Olam Haba*, in the World to Come."

He was a rabbi from the older generation who had watched the erosion of *Yiddishkeit* over the years, and then seen with wonder its resurgence in the youth. He had lost all his relatives in the Holocaust, and had sat far into the night with congregants who were trying to re-establish some kind of faith after tragedy.

He had performed countless *brisin, bar-mitzvahs*, weddings and funerals, and had known the joys and sorrows of people who, though not following in his teachings of *halachah*, had leaned on him emotionally in any time of trouble. He had been there for them, through it all. He had tried to break through the misconception that only the rabbi had to be *frum*, and felt he had not been truly successful in doing so.

He welcomed Mr. Isaacson and his son into his study, noting with satisfaction that the son looked like a *yeshivah bachur*. Seeing young people like that, especially young people who had grown up in Cape Town, warmed his heart.

He listened carefully to their questions.

A wedding that he performed twenty-three years ago. That was difficult, really difficult. Ari told him more about his great- grandmother, and then he suddenly remembered.

"Yes, why yes of course! She was a very frum lady, a very, very *frum* lady. Her grandfather had been one of the great *rosh yeshivos* back in the old country."

In spite of his despair, Ari's heart gave a jump. He would find out more about that later. If only his own birth was proved to be kosher, perhaps he could match Brocha's background, a little. But he must not think of that now. He tried to block it out of his mind.

"This was her grandchild's wedding. A very beautiful one it was too. Sylvie, her name was. That was your mother, wasn't it?"

"Yes," said Ari.

"She married a man called Donald Levine. I think he was a *Levi*. A very nice young man." He looked at Ari's father.

"I am her second husband," he said.

"Was the wedding completely Orthodox?" said Ari, already knowing the answer.

"Absolutely," said the rabbi. "The old lady would never have allowed anything else. She was devastated that her son and his wife were not *frum*, and that they brought up their children with hardly any *Yiddishkeit*. She would come to my *shul* and say *Tehillim* for hours, just for her family."

"When did she die?" asked Ari's father.

"I think it was very shortly after that. I don't remember exactly," said the rabbi.

"My ex-wife was divorced from him. The marriage didn't last long. Was there a *get*?" asked Mr. Isaacson.

"You should know that," said the rabbi. "I mean, you would not have been able to marry her without a *get*."

"We were married in court," said Mr. Isaacson quietly.

The rabbi stiffened. He suddenly looked several years older.

"This young man's mother was Sylvia," the rabbi stammered. "Who is his father?"

"I am," said Mr. Isaacson.

"Let me check out that wedding," said the rabbi. "Let me see if there is a record of a *get*." His hands were trembling.

"Have you any idea when they were divorced?"

Mr. Isaacson gave a vague date about a year after the marriage.

"I will look in the funerals as well," he said. He looked at Ari, an expression of infinite sadness on his face.

"He knows," thought Ari. "He knows what is happening." He felt sick. If only something could be done to ease his pain, to place him back in the realm of being a kosher Jew. But then if he wasn't, he never had been a kosher Jew.

Time seemed to stand still. The hands on the *shul's* ancient clock seemed hardly to move.

After what seemed like an eternity, Rabbi Drotsky was back.

"The wedding was twenty-six years ago," he announced. "It was completely Orthodox. There is no *get* recorded over here, not in the Cape Province, anyway. The grandmother, Gittle Brocha, died three months after the wedding."

"Brocha," said Ari, and then the impact of what the rabbi was saying hit him and he burst into tears. His father too, could only hold back the tears for a minute longer than his son. Even the rabbi found that he had to dry his eyes.

"Rabbi Drotsky," said David Isaacson at last. "Rabbi Drotsky, why didn't you tell us all? Why didn't you tell South African Jewry what could happen if a woman got married without a *get*? We didn't know. We had no idea!"

"All the Orthodox rabbis have been telling South African Jewry. We have been crying about it from the pulpits and writing about it in the Jewish newspapers," he said.

He went to a storeroom at the back of the *shul* and brought back three faded, yellow, Jewish newspapers.

"These," he said, "these and these," he said as he showed them three articles all written by him, begging people to obtain a *get,* and spelling out clearly what the consequences could be if they didn't. Few seem to have ever taken it seriously.

"Then there is no hope left," said Mr. Isaacson.

"Oh yes there is," said the rabbi, straightening up. "There was no *get* given in the Cape Province. But there is the whole of South Africa left, and Zambia and Zimbabwe. There is the whole world. A *get* could have been obtained anywhere. You have to find this Donald Levine. He is the only one who can help you. In the meanwhile, I will start writing to other cities to see if they have any news for you. But . . ."

He looked at Ari.

"But, please would you do just one thing for me?"

"Of course," said Ari, wondering what on earth the rabbi would ask him to do.

"I had a young woman here to see me earlier today," he said. "People in her position come to me quite often. She has a civil divorce, but her husband won't give her a *get* until she pays 5000 rand. She says she won't do it, on principle. Why should she pay him? Why is it so important? She will get married in court or in Reform.

"Ari," he said, "Ari, I told her all the consequences. I am trying to help her, and I offered to negotiate with her husband. She didn't listen to me. She didn't seem to hear at all what I was saying. She doesn't think an antiquated Jewish divorce is worth her life savings, or worth putting up a big fight. She won't listen to me, but perhaps, Ari, she will listen to you and listen to your father. I know you have to get on with your investigations, but please will you speak to her?

"She is a very nice young woman, and is likely to get married again very soon, and then look at the position in which she is placing her children.

"She doesn't know, just like your father didn't know, except that no one even tried to explain it to your father."

Mr. Isaacson had been listening intently.

"Of course we will talk to her. Please phone her and make the appointment. We will come to your office and talk to her. We might be saving the future of a Jewish child. This is important. Ari, this is something I have to do, and, Rabbi, this is something I will continue to do. If anyone comes to you confused or hesitant about a *get*, please contact me."

Thirty-Three

The young woman looked antagonistically at Ari and his father. She was likely to remarry soon, they realized. They had to do something to avert the tragedy of her marrying without obtaining a *get*.

"Mrs. Silberman," began Rabbi Drotsky, "just to indulge the whim of a rabbi who has been serving this community for two-thirds of a century, please, listen to this man and his son. I am not forcing you into anything. I just want you to listen to what they have to say."

The rabbi left and she glared at them, but then she noticed the suffering in both their eyes and, being a sensitive young woman, she felt her anger vanish.

"I don't know why I am supposed to listen to you," she said. "But I will."

She turned to Ari. "You look a bit like an up and coming rabbi," she said. "I hope you're not going to preach to me."

"Don't worry," said Ari. "There will be no sermons. My father is going to tell you our story. I will just add in the small pieces."

"All right," she said, smiling. "Go ahead and tell me."

David Isaacson cleared his throat.

"It's about this young man here, my son, Anthony, though now he calls himself Ari, his Hebrew name."

"It all started off in an ambulance flying down the road on the South Coast of Natal. The sirens were screaming. On a stretcher, surrounded by the paramedics, is a woman, my ex-wife. In a seat in a corner of the ambulance is a young boy of twelve, my son, Anthony."

Ari was stunned at the talent his father had in telling a story. Even though he was in fact the hero of the story, he listened, enthralled, as if he had never heard it before. He marvelled at how his father had been aware of his inner feelings.

As he spoke on and on, sparing nothing, Ari looked at his father with a new admiration and respect. He put everything he had into convincing this woman that she had to obtain a *get*, and yet all he was doing was telling a story, a story about himself and his son, and how they seemed to have got themselves caught up into something irreversible.

The woman smiled when he spoke about Brocha, the wonderful daughter of the *rosh yeshivah*, and she congratulated Ari. Her reaction however, made what was to follow even more painful and she listened with horror as to what had happened and what was happening.

When Mr. Isaacson had finished, she was crying.

"I never understood," she said. "I never, ever understood. None of my friends understands this. Oh yes, the rabbi spelled it out clearly; he said exactly what you said, but I never understood what it could really mean. I don't know why not, but I didn't hear.

"Ari," she said, "I want you to know that what has happened to you is going to save all my future children. I didn't say it to the rabbi, but there is already someone I am thinking of marrying. He wouldn't have minded if I had got married in a Reform service, or even in court. He would never have thought about a *get*. Whatever happens, I am going to get a *get* as soon as possible, no matter how much it costs me. I see now that this is far, far more important than anything money can buy, and if money can buy it, one should rush to take the opportunity. The rabbi is going to help me, which I appreciate.

"Some of my friends could have gotten a *get* for nothing, and they didn't even bother to do so. I am going to speak to them and if necessary, I might ask you, Mr. Isaacson, to speak to them. If they won't listen to me, I will get them together and invite you and your wife, and Ari, if he is still here, to come over and put it across to them. They have got to know!"

Ari called in the rabbi, and the woman repeated some of what she had said to him. He was thrilled beyond words.

"You see," he said to Ari and his father as they were leaving, "you have done an extremely important *mitzvah*. Maybe you have started something in this community. Maybe we need not all despair for this situation."

They turned to go and he called them back.

"Wait," he said, "I have a lead for you to follow up. No, I still haven't found that your mother had a *get*," he said as he saw Ari's look of expectation. "But I found the application forms for her first marriage. At the time, Donald Levine was working at Stan's jewelers. He might still be in the trade. Perhaps we could trace him through that."

When Ari and his father got home, they were surprised to find Sheila, Yehudah and even Debby looking quite excited.

"Mummy bought new dishes," said Debby. "Look how pretty. Two sets, one for milk and one for meat. We can't use them yet until our house is *kashered*, but Zevi's mother and father will help us with it. We all went over to their house to look in their cupboards to see what we could or couldn't eat."

In spite of his situation, Ari found himself becoming very excited. He had to look at the positive side of the situation. If this hadn't happened to him, the woman they had just met might have had several children who were not kosher Jews. Also, his stepmother would never have changed her house to become kosher, he was sure. Perhaps all this was meant to be.

But oh, how he longed for the nightmare to be finished. How he longed for something, somewhere, to prove that he was a kosher Jew.

Later, when Ari and Yehudah had gone for *Minchah* and *Maariv* and a *shiur* at the Levy's, and when Debby was busy with her homework in her room, Sheila spoke to her husband.

"I think I did a *mitzvah* today," she said.

"I am sure you did," he said warmly. "I am so, so proud of what you did."

"How do you know what I did?" she asked.

"Well, the plates are all ready and the kitchen has that expectant look," he said, smiling.

"No, I'm not talking about that," she said. "I went to my book club. There was a woman there who is getting remarried, and she was saying to a friend of hers that the wedding would have to be Reform even though she did prefer the Orthodox service. Why? Because all those years ago, she didn't get a *get*."

"Did you speak to her?" he asked.

"Of course I did," she said. "I didn't mention, of course, that it was my stepson that this happened to; I said it was a relative. The women were hanging onto my every word, and every so often they would given an exclamation of horror. The woman thanked me and said she would set about straightaway to get a *get*. She had not thought it was even really worth bothering about."

Yaakov phoned that evening.

"How is everything going?" he asked. "Have you found out anything yet?"

"We have found out things that make the situation worse," said Ari. "But we still have leads to follow up. We are trying," he said.

"But Yaakov," he said, before his friend could sympathize, "such amazing things have happened. Aunt Sheila is making the home kosher, and Yehudah is allowed as much contact as he wants with your family. Also," he added, "Aunt Sheila and Dad have been doing quite a lot to explain to people the importance of a *get*."

"That's fantastic," said Yaakov, amazed at the change in his friend. How could he sound so happy when it had been established beyond doubt that the marriage to Donald Levine was a kosher one?

But he wasn't happy about his own status. He was looking at the changes in his family and their influence for good on others. Ari was a very special person. Whatever his position, he could remain a very special person, and, kosher or not, a very special Jew.

Thirty-Four

Stan's was an exclusive shop right in the center of the city. They specialized in engagement rings, gold and precious jewelery and fine watches. There was no way one could buy rolled gold, semi-precious stones or costume jewelery in such a shop. There was also no way one could leave with anything from the shop without paying in the thousands.

As Ari and his father entered the shop, a well-dressed young man came towards them, inquiring what they might be interested in.

"We don't want to buy anything," said Mr. Isaacson. "We just want to inquire about someone who used to work here many, many years ago."

"How long ago would that be?" asked the man.

"Around twenty-five or twenty-six years ago," said Mr. Isaacson.

The man looked at him suspiciously. "How old do I look?" he asked a little sharply, and then he controlled himself. After all, he was a salesman and he had to be cordial at all times.

"I am afraid we don't have records going that far back." He turned to Ari.

"Young man, you will probably be thinking of getting engaged one day. You will want to get a ring. Could I show you some that we have in the shop? They are the best quality, and although we keep the highest standards, our prices are very competitive."

He looked straight at Ari and was suddenly struck by the pain in his eyes.

Ari and his father thanked him and began to go out of the shop.

"Wait a minute," said the salesman. "There is someone who might be able to help you. We have an older man working at our other branch. He is nearly eighty. He should have retired years ago, but he is one of the best salesmen we have ever had. He actually has a phenomenal memory. He might remember this person you are looking for."

He handed him a card with the address of both shops.

"Mr. McPherson, his name is. You can't miss him. He will probably also try to sell this young man an engagement ring, and he might succeed. He could sell the Eiffel Tower if he put his mind to it."

They left the shop, thanking him. Ari was very quiet.

"I felt for you, Anthony," said his father. "The word 'engaged' must set off a bad reaction. You know, Anthony, you are still engaged. Brocha knows nothing about this, does she?"

"No, but she will have to, because I won't be able to stay engaged to her." His voice trembled. "I would so love to marry her," he said. "There just isn't another person like her anywhere."

"I just have a feeling that you are going to marry her," said Mr. Isaacson.

"Don't say that, Dad, I can't bear it. I don't want to think about it. We mustn't talk about it."

"I know, Anthony, I am sorry," said his father. "Here is the car," he said as he found the parking lot. "We have to go to the west side of town for the other branch. It is too far to walk. We will find a Parkade or something there."

Driving in town was never his favorite, and he tried to contain his irritation with double or even triple parked vehicles which seemed intent on blocking his way.

It took half an hour to get through the traffic.

"It would have been quicker to walk," he remarked as he found a parking place with a meter. He gave a groan as he saw that it was out of order.

"We will risk the cops just this once," he said. "There's Stan's right over there. We can't get a parking ticket in ten minutes."

They went into the shop, disappointed that they were being served by a young woman.

"We wanted to speak to Mr. McPherson," said Ari.

"He won't be in this morning, can I help you?"

Ari was disappointed. "No thank you," he said. "We wanted to ask him about someone who worked here many years ago. I am not here to buy anything."

The young woman shrugged her shoulders.

At that moment Mr. Isaacson looked out of the window and saw a traffic officer working his way down the street. In another two minutes he would be right by his car.

"Anthony," he called, "I will be right back. There's a cop right by the car. I don't want a ticket." With that he was gone.

"I had better wait for him," said Ari. "If I go he won't know where I am."

"He'll have a lot of difficulty finding parking here," she said, "but he might be lucky."

Ari looked at some of the jewelery. This shop seemed a little less exclusive than the city shop, and they stocked the less expensive items as well.

Where was his father? How long would he take?

"When will Mr. McPherson be back? What time this afternoon?"

She hesitated. "Actually he is here," she said. "He just isn't feeling well. He gets these turns sometimes, but he can't tell his employers because they might fire him. I am sure you can speak to him."

"Yes, yes of course he can come," a rather squeaky voice came from the back. "Come here, boy. How can I help you?"

Ari stepped into the back room, amazed at the difference between the wood and velvet panelled shop on the one side and the tiny brick room behind it with a stark washbasin and two old stools.

"I want to find someone called Donald Levine," he said. "He was working for Stan's around twenty-five or twenty-six years ago."

"Oh, those were the days," said the little, white-haired man whose eyes seemed to squint, possibly from his years and years of examining jewelery. "I remember Cape Town twenty-five years ago. People had respect then. Now they don't. People knew what real jewelery was. Now they buy the utmost rubbish. Cubic Zerconium indeed. They may as well be buying glass. Oh, I know you can't tell the difference, but I can, and the person who owns it knows what it is and knows it isn't a real diamond. They relate to it like that, they do.

"A diamond has a warmth and a sparkle and a fire inside it. A real fire it has. These imitations are like electricity. Man-made, not the real thing. Have you seen the difference between a rose and the most beautifully made artificial one? You might be proud of your artificial one, but you know the difference, you know it's not real."

"That's true," said Ari. He wished the man would answer his question. Had he heard his question?

He was about to ask it again, when the man went on.

"Even cars in those days were better. They were good and sound and reliable. Today everything is throw-away, everything is polystyrene. Not cars, of course, but everything else. You get watches that are so cheap they aren't even worth repairing. Real rubbish, I call them. We don't stock them, of course, but no one appreciates a real watch any more. They go for these cheap, fancy, gaudy things.

"Oh, the world has changed. But it was changing even in those days. Your friend Donald Levine and I used to have long discussions about it. He was much younger than I was, so he tried to defend these new-fangled inventions. But even he had to admit that not all of them were progress, especially in the jewelery trade."

"Do you know where Donald Levine might be now?" asked Ari, hoping he could distract him from his monologue.

"Have no idea, no idea at all," he said. "He left years ago, right up North, then he came back and left again. And young man, I want you to scrutinize every bit of jewelery you buy. There are too many unscrupulous people in the trade. You can trust me, though. People have known for years that they can trust me. If you want anything, come to me. I can guarantee whatever I sell you. If you come to me, it will be the real thing.

"Some of my not too honest colleagues might be passing off cubes as diamonds. I have no proof though, no proof at all. I just think they might be. It is difficult to tell if you don't know how.

"Now, don't tell anyone I have said these things. I don't want to get taken to court or anything." He shivered a little.

"I think Donald went to Durban, maybe even to our branch over there. Once a jeweler, always a jeweler. So if he isn't at Stan's, he will be somewhere else, in Katz's or one of the many other jewelers. He was a good salesman if ever there was one. Always said he wanted to go into his own business, but few of us manage to do that. Maybe he did."

At that moment Ari's father rushed into the shop.

"Come with me, Anthony, we will be back later to speak to the gentleman. I have double-parked outside. There is a policeman still floating around, so please come now."

Apologizing and thanking Mr. McPherson profusely, Ari left the shop and climbed quickly into his father's car.

"When will the man be in?" Mr. Isaacson asked.

"He was in," said Ari. "I spoke to him, or rather, he spoke to me."

"Oh, I am sorry to rush you then," said his father. "I thought you were just waiting for me."

"You rescued me," said Ari, giving a sigh of relief. "He could have talked for hours and hours."

"And Donald Levine?" asked his father.

"Durban," said Ari. "He went to Durban. He went to Stan's in Durban, and may be there or at one of the other jewelers. He might even be in his own business. As Mr. McPherson says, 'Once a jeweler, always a jeweler.'"

"Durban," said Mr. Isaacson thoughtfully. "I suppose we had to end up going to Durban together again. We will make all the arrangements and leave very early tomorrow morning."

Thirty-Five

They left very early that morning, long before sunrise. Ari told his father that they would have to stop and *daven* somewhere on the road. He even brought the compass he usually travelled with, so that he could work out the direction in which he could *daven*.

"Stop the car, please, Dad. I need to *daven*. Maybe you can read a book or something until I have finished, and have some of those cookies the Levys made for us."

"Don't worry about me, my boy," said his father. "I will sleep a while. Please take as long as you like. I am quite comfortable."

Almost as if to confirm what he was saying, he closed his eyes.

He must in fact have dozed somewhat, because when he came to he looked towards his son and found him in the middle of his *davening*. He was wearing *tefillin*, and as he *davened* from his tiny *siddur*, he was swaying back and forth. Mr. Isaacson watched him, fascinated. Was this holy man his son?

Ari looked so entranced by what he was doing.

Could he really be communicating with Hashem, Mr. Isaacson wondered. Is that what *davening* was really about? As he looked at his son, he realized there were tears flowing down his cheeks, but he didn't look sad or desperate. Ari was totally absorbed in the *davening*.

Mr. Isaacson had always seen *davening* as reading, or rather, breaking your teeth, on a lot of rather difficult Hebrew words. This looked like something different, something alive and meaningful.

For a moment he was gripped by a strange emotion—jealousy! But he wasn't jealous of his son. How could he possibly be! Well, in a way he was; he was jealous because his son could put on *tefillin* and *daven*, and he couldn't. But what was really stopping him? Well, he couldn't, could he? He hadn't done it before, except at his *bar-mitzvah*, and then he had felt something. Hadn't he? That had meant something to him.

He reached over to the plastic bag in front of him and took one of the cookies.

Delicious, they were. Those Levys knew how to cook. He quickly ate it and reached for a second one, at the same time never taking his eyes off his son, as if mesmerized by him.

Eventually he felt the bag. It was becoming rather empty. In fact, there were hardly any cookies left.

What would Sheila say? She was always telling him to be careful with his weight. But he wouldn't be home for a couple of days, and maybe she wouldn't notice.

Ari finished *davening* and started to wrap up his *tefillin*. Well, it was now, or probably never. He got out of the car.

"Ari, son," he said rather apologetically. "Do you think you could show me how to put those things on? I mean, just for a minute?"

"Of course, Dad," said Ari, looking delighted. "Do you know the *Shema Yisrael*?"

"I used to," said his father. "I don't think I do any more."

"Give me a few minutes, Dad," said Ari. "I am going to write out the first line in phonetic Hebrew in English letters, and the rest of it in English, so that you can read it. Then I will show you what to do."

"By the way," said his father, "I think I ate up most of the cookies. I was sort of nervous, thinking about Donald Levine and everything."

"Don't worry, Dad," said Ari. "The Levys gave us an incredible amount of food, and so did Yehudah. We won't starve at all."

"Good people, the Levys," said his father. "You know, I was very against the Levys at first because of their strong influence on you and Jules, but I see now they are very good friends, perhaps the best friends we have ever had."

For some reason, Ari insisted on their booking into the beachfront hotel in which they were together so many years ago, just after his mother had died, this time without meals, of course.

It was not long before they were in Stan's West Street City Branch. Again they drew a blank. No one seemed to be able to give them any information about someone who had been there twenty years before.

Was this again going to be so difficult?

"Perhaps we could just visit all the city jewelers and see if we can find him," said Ari. "We have to find him, Dad. We have to find him."

They spent almost that whole day trudging from one jeweler to another, but no one seemed to have employed such a person.

It was getting close to five o'clock, closing time, and they were both becoming extremely depressed, until they came to Katz's jewelers.

The man behind the counter shook his head. "Donald Levine? No, we haven't had anyone working for us by that name."

They turned to go out when he called them back.

"But wait a minute, wouldn't he be from Levine's Jewelers?"

"He could be," said Ari. "He said that he would one day be going into his own business."

"Well, it's been in existence for at least fifteen years," said the man. "I am almost sure the owner there is Donald Levine. Levine it definitely is, otherwise why the name?"

"We will go there right away," said Ari.

"Well, that will be difficult," said the man. "I am just about to close up, and they are several streets away. You will probably have to wait until tomorrow morning to find him. He will open at around nine o'clock."

They asked for exact directions to the store, and made their way there. It was definitely the right store, as it had Donald Levine's name painted discreetly on one corner of the window. However, it was barred and locked with not even a hint of the number of where the owner could be contacted.

"We've found him anyway," said Mr. Isaacson. "We can come here straightaway tomorrow morning and settle everything."

Ari was shivering. "You realize that my whole future probably rests on this."

"I know, son," said his father. "Son, I prayed for you this morning, all the time I had those straps tied all over me. After I read the *Shema*, I was praying for you. Hashem must have been really surprised to hear from me after so long. Maybe He will listen, and we will find out that your mother had a *get* and everything will be all right."

"Thanks, Dad," said Ari.

They walked around the shops, window-shopping together. At times they even enjoyed it, but most of the time their minds were preoccupied with what they would find the next day.

"Ari," said his father, "if all this hadn't happened and you had just married Brocha and everything had gone quite smoothly, I don't think we would have all become involved like this. Maybe it was supposed to happen, just to, as it were, get us also onto the train. But now we are getting there, so it is time you found your mother's *get* and got on with your engagement."

Ari stifled a cry to his father to stop hurting him so deeply. He didn't mean it, he knew, but Ari had already braced himself for Donald Levine very apologetically saying that there had been no *get*. She hadn't asked for one, had she?

He was beginning to feel the old depression and anxiety.

"Let's walk along the beach, Dad," he said. "There won't be anyone swimming any more. It's getting dark. Let's look at the Fun Fair and the computer games. I want to see if I can still play them."

They caught a bus down West Street to South Beach. They had left their car parked at the hotel. David Isaacson had no intention of getting on the wrong side of the Durban traffic cops this time. It was far easier to walk and to take a bus, if necessary. The sun was beginning to set, and the sky would have inspired any artist.

"You know," said Ari, "it is almost exactly ten years since we were together on this beachfront and yet, though there are many, many differences, in some ways everything is the same."

He pointed to the Fun Fair.

"That's the same, except that they have added some water rides. We won't go on those."

His father followed rather gingerly as Ari made his way around the ferris wheel, the merry-go-round and the large boats. They walked till they came to an entrance which read "Ghost Train Ride of Horrors."

"I'm taking you for a ride, Dad," said Ari, a mischievous smile on his face. "Come, I'll pay for you."

He bought two tickets and they sat in a mechanical car. Suddenly, it whizzed through a horror hall of ghosts, skeletons and slimy things which suddenly caught on one's face. Both Ari and his father screamed and laughed from beginning to end.

"My turn to take you," said Ari's father when they had finished. He purchased the tickets and once more they laughingly got into the car.

No less than eight times was this repeated until Ari and his father made their exhausted way home.

"I'll *daven Maariv*, and then I'll put out supper," said Ari. "Don't worry. I don't have to cook anything, everything is ready-to-eat," he said. "Tomorrow I will know more or less where I stand. But in the meanwhile, let's enjoy today!"

Thirty-Six

"Sorry to keep you waiting, but we don't open until nine o'clock." The man who came to open the shop looked at them apologetically. "And it is only ten to nine," he added, looking carefully at his watch.

"I know that," said Mr. Isaacson. "I only wanted some information from you. I wanted to speak to Mr. Donald Levine. I believe he is the owner of this business."

"Not any more, sir," said the man. "It used to belong to him. That's why it's called Levine's Jewelers. Now it belongs to my father, but we didn't change the name because it is a good name, and people know it by that.

"Mr. Levine sold out and retired three years ago because of illness."

Both Ari and his father held their breath. Eventually Ari spoke.

"Have you any idea where he lives?" he asked.

"Oh, yes," said the man. "Just wait until I have opened up properly and I'll give you the address and the phone number, if you like."

Twenty minutes later, they were knocking on Donald Levine's door. Ari was excited but nervous. His father looked somewhat pessimistic.

"Don't raise your hopes too high," he was saying. "We will find out what we can."

A middle-aged woman opened the door and looked at them a little suspiciously through the safety grill.

"We would like to speak to Mr. Donald Levine," said Mr. Isaacson.

"I'm sorry, that won't be possible," said the woman.

"I must speak to him. It is really important," said Mr. Isaacson.

The woman looked at him strangely.

"I am sorry, but he passed away a few months ago," she said.

Ari immediately burst into tears and turned away from the door.

Mr. Isaacson looked devastated.

"What is the matter? Can I help you?" the woman asked. These people were obviously upset, extremely upset. But why did the death of her husband affect them so much? She didn't remember them ever visiting him. Were they perhaps friends, good friends that she didn't know about? And they looked like decent people. In fact the young man, who was obviously the son, looked rather like a rabbi.

She could not understand why he should be crying, why he should be so distressed, and she knew she could not just leave it. She was a motherly person, having sons of her own. This boy was very upset and needed help. They were both upset.

"Please come in," she said, unlocking the safety door. "I can see something is troubling you very, very deeply. Please come in."

Not really knowing what else to do, they accepted the invitation. After all, she might know some relatives of Donald Levine who might know if there was a *get*. But both father and son felt their search had ended. They had failed. The only man who could help them was dead.

"Please tell me what is worrying you. Perhaps I can help," the woman said.

She kept insisting, until, feeling that it could not do much harm, father and son between them, told the whole story. By the end, both were crying.

The woman went out of the room and came back several minutes later with a large, brown envelope.

"I will show you something soon, but now I will tell you my story.

"I am Mrs. Deidre Levine. My husband was Donald Levine. He was married before to your mother, Sylvia Shapiro." She looked at Ari who had his eyes fixed on hers.

"My boy, of course your mother had a *get*. Do you think I would marry a man who was still married to someone else according to Jewish law?"

Ari's face had gone a chalky white. Was he dreaming? Could this be true?

"I couldn't have married a man who hadn't given his wife a *get*. I might not be *frum*, but I know what is right and wrong. Did you ever read Rabbi Drotsky's articles? He spells everything out, clearly and simply.

"I insisted on a *get*, though I must admit it was a few months later. How old are you, son?" she asked.

"Twenty-two, nearly twenty-three," said Ari, hardly daring to breathe.

"I married Donald Levine in an Orthodox *shul*, three years before you were born. My oldest son is two years older than you. He is married, and I have two grandchildren, such beautiful children, beautiful children like you and Brocha will have."

Tears were now running freely down Ari's face, but his eyes were shining.

"Look in this envelope," she said. "You can take that *get* document. You will need it. My marriage certificate and *Ketubah* you can give back to me. We needed the *get* to be able to get it."

He looked at all of them. To him these were documents that radiated life. Had they fallen straight out of heaven?

Some time later, they rose to leave.

"I have to make some phone calls," he said.

"If you would like to phone your rabbis, it would give me infinite satisfaction if you could phone them from here. I am so happy about this, I want to share it a little with you." She led him to the phone.

Ari dialed the number and got straight through to Rabbi Weinstein.

As calmly as he could, he said, "Rabbi, I want to read a certain document to you, signed and sealed by the *Beis Din* of Salisbury, then Southern Rhodesia, now Zimbabwe, dated three years before I was born. Let me start from the beginning."

Thirty-Seven

It was a wedding full of *simchah*, all the guests remarking that there was certainly something special about it, without being able to say what it was.

Was it the radiance and the happiness of the couple themselves? Or was it their good looks that struck people?

Was it the joy of Rabbi and Rebbetzin Goldstein and their family? Or was it the sincerity of increasing commitment to *Yiddishkeit* in the *chassan's* family? Their younger son, Yehudah, certainly looked like a *yeshivah bachur*, and wasn't he attending the Yeshivah High School?

Was it the undiluted joy of Rabbi Weinstein who had made the *shidduch* and who had been sent a ticket to England by the *kallah's* parents?

Or was it the happiness of Rabbi Levy and his two sons, Yaakov and Zevi? Yaakov would be learning in a *yeshivah* in England, and his father had come with him to make final arrangements and, of course, to attend the wedding.

How had Zevi afforded to come to England? He had been teaching his dyslexic pupil very conscientiously and had refused any remuneration. The boy had done so well that his father, who worked for South African Airways, had seen to it that Zevi was handed a ticket with a seat number next to Yehudah, right behind his father and brother.

And of course there were all the *roshei yeshivah* and rabbis from England who found themselves delighted with the *shidduch.*

Ari had spoken at length to Rabbi Drotsky, who had eventually remembered who Ari's great-great-great-grandfather was, and a little research had come up with very rewarding results. He had been a *rosh yeshivah* in Lithuania.

At the end of the wedding, Rabbi Goldstein said to his son-in-law, "You've travelled far, very far to get here Ari. I am proud of you. This day is one of the happiest days of my life."

As he looked at his father-in-law and saw the happiness and the *kedushah* radiating from his face, Ari wondered what he would think if he really knew how far he had come or what he had been through to get here.

It could have been a tragedy for all of them. But there had been a *get.* That had been established beyond a shadow of a doubt, and both Rabbi Weinstein and Rabbi Levy felt that it was not necessary to tell the Goldsteins what could have been.

Perhaps one day he would tell Brocha, but today, nothing would or could mar their happiness.

He met his father-in-law's eyes, and smiled.

Glossary

alef-beis: Hebrew alphabet
baal teshuvah: penitent
bachur(im): youth(s)
bar-mitzvah: halachic adulthood
Baruch Hashem: Blessed is the Name; thank Heaven
bentch: bless [Yiddish]
bentcher: booklet containing Grace after Meals
bris: covenant
chalav: milk
Chanukah: Festival of lights
chas veshalom: Heaven forbid
chassan: bridegroom
chavrusa: study partner
Chevrah Kadishah: burial society
Chumash: Book of the Pentateuch
chuppah: bridal canopy
daven: pray
eidim: witnesses
frum: observant [Yiddish]
Gemara: part of the Talmud
ger: convert to Judaism
get: bill of Jewish divorce
glatt: strictly kosher
haftorah: supplementary Torah reading
Halachah: the body of Jewish law
havdalah: concluding ritual of *Shabbos*
hechsherim: endorsements
heter: permissive ruling
kallah: bride
kashered: made kosher
kashrus: state of being kosher
kedushah: holiness
Ketubah: nuptial agreement
kiddush: santification of Shabbos or festivals
Kislev: Jewish month, roughly corresponding to December
l'chaim: to life, traditional toast
licht: candles
Limudei Kodesh: sacred studies
Maariv: evening prayer
matzoh: unleavened bread
Mazel tov: congratulations
mechinah: intermediate Torah school

melamdim: teachers
menorah: candelabra
mezuzah: scroll affixed to doorpost
midos: character traits
Minchah: afternoon service
minyan: quorum of ten
Mishnayos: part of the Talmud
mitzvos: Torah commandments
Motzei Shabbos: night after the Shabbos
neshamah: soul
Nissan: Jewish month, roughly corresponding to April
Olam Haba: the world to come
parshah: portion of the Torah
parve: neither meat nor dairy
pasuk: verse
Pesach: Passover, early spiring festival
pilpul: involved Torah presentation
rav: rabbi
rosh yeshivah: dean
Rosh Hashanah: New year; tractate of the Talmud
sedarim: Passover feasts
sefarim: books
semichah: Rabbinical ordination
Shabbaton: large *Shabbos* gathering
Shabbos: the Sabbath; tractate of the Talmud
Shema: Jewish confession of faith
sheva brachos: the Seven Nuptial Blessings
shidduch: match
shiur: lecture
Shemoneh Esrei: the Eighteen Benedictions, fundamental part of daily prayers
shul: synagogue [Yiddish]
Siddur: prayer book
simchah: rejoicing
talmid chacham: Torah scholar
tefillin: phylacteries
yarmulka: skullcap
yeshivah gedolah: advanced
yeshivah: torah school
yichus: distinguished lineage
Yiddishkeit: Jewishness
Yom Kippur: Day of Atonement
Yom Tov: festival